WHATEVER HAPPENED TO LIAM MCLYN?

DAVID B. LYONS

 ISBN: 978-1-7398552-6-0

Created with Vellum

LIAM

I look at him. And he looks at me. And he smiles. And then he stares straight ahead again. To look at the road. So, I look out the passenger side window, and I start to think he might not be going the right way.

'It's. The. Grand. Hotel,' I say. And when I say it I know I sound funny, because I change my voice when I am talking to someone from a different country. I speak slower. And more careful. So that they understand me. I spoke that way with the football coach who was teaching us this morning.

'Yes,' the man says. 'This is the right way.'

It seems I am longer in his car than I would have been walking. But I was happy for the lift. Because I had been playing football for a long, long time and my feet needed a rest. And I wanted to get back to the hotel as quickly as possible. Because me and Mammy and Daddy and Yvonne are going to the Prague Zoo today.

I was looking around the corner to make sure it was the right way to turn when this man pulled over in his blue car. And asked if I was lost.

'Is The Grand Hotel this turn?' I asked him. Even though I

knew it was. He smiled at me. And he looked nice and helpful when he smiled. Even though his face was covered by a bushy beard.

'It's uh,' he said. Then he leaned over and opened his passenger door. 'Let me drive you back to The Grand Hotel. It's not far.'

My dad never lets me sit in the front passenger seat of his car back home. So I was excited. And got into the blue car. But now I think I shouldn't have got in. The man is driving me the wrong way. This is definitely the wrong way.

'Are you sure?' I ask. 'I thought the hotel was closer than this...'

'I'm just showing you a bit more of this beautiful city,' the man says. 'Don't worry, boy.'

I try not to worry. Even when the white houses we were driving around turn to grey houses and it looks like we are getting further away from where the hotel is.

'It's just...' I say, looking up at him again. 'My mammy and daddy are taking me and my sister to Prague Zoo this morning. They said we could go when I got back to the hotel after I did my football practice. They didn't want me to do the football practice this morning. But I begged and begged. And I promised I'd get back to the hotel as early as I could.'

He looks at me and smiles behind his beard again. He looks friendly. Really friendly. But I wish I had have just walked back to the hotel. And not gone on a drive looking around the city.

'We won't be long,' he says. 'Two more minutes.'

He keeps driving. Turning onto more streets that are all grey and not bright white which is what the hotel is. The hotel is really bright white. As if it was painted white yesterday. And probably the day before that. That's what my dad said on the first day of our holiday.

'They must paint Prague every day.'

I wasn't sure if he was joking. Because the buildings do look like they've been painted every day. But my mammy laughed, and then I knew my daddy was only joking.

'Where are you from, boy?' the man asks.

'Ireland,' I say. 'I'm from County Cork, ever heard of it?'

'Yes, of course,' he says. 'Roy Keane.'

'Yeah,' I say. 'Roy Keane and Denis Irwin. I'm from the same town as Denis Irwin. Near Turners Cross. Do you know who Denis Irwin is?'

'Of course,' he says.

'Are you a Manchester United fan?' I ask.

'I am a Benfica fan,' he says.

'Benfica?' I say. 'Portugal?'

'Yes,' he says.

'Why do you support them?' I ask.

'I am from Portugal,' he says. 'When I was a young boy like you, I lived just outside Benfica.'

'Ohhh,' I say.

'You support Manchester United, yes?' he says. I look down at the crest on my jersey. 'Course,' I say.

'Tell me, what is your age, boy?' he asks. 'Nine,' I tell him. 'I'll be ten in November.'

'Oh,' he says.

Then he pulls the car over to the side of the road and when he turns the key and the engine goes off, I stare up at him at first. Then back out the passenger side window.

'I need to get to the hotel. My mammy and daddy—' I say. And when I say it I think I might cry. Just a little bit. So I stop talking...

'I won't keep you long,' he says. 'I just need to get something from my house. For you. A football that I think you would like. It was signed by Eusebio.'

'Eusebio?'

'Yeah.... Eusebio. One of the greatest footballers of all time,' he says.

I shrug my shoulder.

'Not better than Ronaldo,' I say.

'No, course not,' he says. 'Only Lionel Messi is better than Ronaldo.'

He turns around, opens his car door and steps out. And he pauses, looking up and down the street before walking around the car, to the passenger side door.

'Ronaldo is better than Messi,' I say as soon as he opens it.

'Shhhh,' he whispers, putting his finger to his lips. 'You need to be very quiet around here okay?'

'Okay,' I say. 'But uh... can we go back to the hotel after you give me the football?'

He smiles. And nods.

'Yes,' he says.

He pulls the door open wider and I get out of the car to get the football. The football signed by ... by ...

'What's the name of the footballer who signed—?'

'Shhhhh,' he says. Like the way my teacher shouts 'shhhh', at me at school. And I feel bad. Bad because he asked me to be quiet and I couldn't stop asking questions. My daddy says that to me all the time. That I don't stop asking questions.

'Jesus, Liam,' he says lots and lots. 'You'll make a fine journalist one day.'

I think I might be one when I grow up. A journalist. If I don't make it as a professional footballer. I might set up my own fan channel on YouTube. Or I'd be a fireman. Being a fireman seems like a cool job. But a professional footballer first. If that doesn't work out, I'll set up a YouTube channel called Liam's Analysis. And if that doesn't work out, I'll be a fireman. A really brave fireman.

He walks to a door that used to be blue but is faded now with a faded number seventy-eight on it and steps up on to a concrete step to open it. When I look inside I see that his house is small. Really small. He has two chairs like ones we have at the small kitchen table. And a tiny TV on the ground. Much smaller than the TV I have in my bedroom.

He looks poor. Poorer than he looked when he smiled at me. When he smiled at me, I thought he looked happy. But his house looks sad.

'Come in,' he says, opening the door wider. 'The football is upstairs.'

I stare straight up the stairs. They're really small and skinny. Like the stairs to our attic.

'I think I would like to go to the hotel... please,' I say. And I step towards the door. But he closes it. And I think I feel scared. I can feel it, in my belly.

'No, please,' he says. 'Let's get that football. Signed by Eusebio.... After you.' He points up the stairs. 'And then... I'll drive you straight back to the hotel. Hey, how old is your father?' he asks.

'Thirty-four. No thirty-six. My mam's thirty-four,' I say.

'Your father will know who Eusebio is. You could give the football to your father as a gift. He'd love that.'

I look up the tiny stairs. Then back at him. And he doesn't look so friendly. Not anymore. He's not smiling. And his face has changed.

'I'll follow you,' I say. I am scared. I know I am. But I'd be more scared if he was following me up the stairs. So I tell him that he has to go first.

He walks up the first wooden step and it creaks. Loud. But the second one he steps on doesn't creak. And then I follow him. On to the creaky first step. And I think I remember my grandad talking about Eusebio... one time. A long time ago. When grandad was alive.

'Is this your house?' I ask.

'It is,' he says.

And when he reaches the landing at the top, he turns around and whispers to me.

'Boy, you sure do ask a lot of questions... C'mon.'

He walks to the door at the back of his small house. And opens it wide to let me walk through.

As soon as I walk inside my belly tells me I'm scared. Really scared. Because all I can see is a small light. On the bed. And when I step closer to the light, I see it is lighting up a face. A girl's face. Her eyes are really round. And really wide. And she's mumbling. Mumbling because there's black tape across her mouth.

'I'm so sorry,' he says from behind me. 'But I have no choice...'

Then I feel Sellotape across my mouth...

LENNY

14:25pm

Lenny tries to take a step forward, only to stagger—his right foot giving way before his left foot sweeps to the side, taking his weight before he has to slap two palms to the grey wall for balance.

'Holy fucking shit,' he whispers.

They're the only words he has managed to mutter since he stumbled, stunned, out of Ruthgar Bilic's dank and dirty home, then around the corner of Ladza Street to where he is stood now, stumbling, stuttering, talking to a wall.

He composes himself by lengthening his breaths, then he glides along the wall like a crab until he reaches the very edge. From there, he pokes his face around the corner to peer the length of Ladza Street, noticing all is quiet again, the door of number twenty-two closed, Ruthgar Bilic back inside his humble home probably still laughing at the pathetic, lost 'investigator'.

'I'm only out of prison two days and you think I'm swiping girls. Get out of my house, you mother fucker!'

Lenny can't stop hearing the thick Czech accent. Over and over again. The laugh more gouging than the false accusation.

He holds his hands over his ears and swivels before stuttering forward, sliding his pointed shoes across the concrete... Moving on. Trying to move on.

He feels another self-punch to the gut, his mind whirs, his own voice calling. Shouting.

'Sofie! Sofie!'

Screaming her name around Bilic's tiny home.

It's not the first time he embarrassed himself in that exact same way. Five years ago he called out Betsy's name in an innocent man's home, too, certain she was in there when she couldn't have been.

He pinches his shoulders together, wincing as he shuffles forward.

'Uuuugh!' Lenny pours the groan out of his mouth as another cringe wiggles his spine, then he washes a hand over his face. Yet he can't stop hearing it. Bilic's laugh. Goading him. Teasing him. Screaming out Lenny's biggest insecurity. 'You're a shit investigator!' Suddenly, Lenny's legs give way, and he drops, his bony ass slapping to the kerb, his wiry legs stretching to the road in front of him, crossing at the ankle.

He leans to one side, shovels his hand into the pocket of his yellow puffer jacket and pulls out his phone before tapping at it. As he stretches it out in front of his bald head, a strange tone trills.

'Hul-ho,' she says, her smiling face blinking on to the screen.

'Celina,' he says, dipping his head, staring down at the grey pavement between his thighs to see another miraculous leaf growing out of a small crack. 'I, uh... I don't think I'm cut out for this.'

'Cut out for... what does this phrase mean, Len-ny?'

'Cut out for... I don't think I'm good at this stuff. At investigating...'

As the line falls silent, Lenny looks up and then down the grey street lined by grey houses, his stomach swallowing nothing.

'What do you mean no good at investigating? You have been finding children since before I have known you.'

'Ahhh, Celina,' Lenny says, scratching the stubble above his ear, then finally facing the friendly face on the screen. 'I just spent the last ten minutes in a house shouting out the missing girl's name. She wasn't there. Sofie wasn't where I thought she was. I got it wrong. I got it wrong again!'

There's another silence on the line, more ominous this time, as if Celina doesn't quite know what to say... Instead, she sucks in her cheeks, holding them between her teeth while she stews...

'All investigators get it wrong, Len-ny,' she finally offers. 'Until they get it right.'

'What?' Lenny says, squinting the length of the grey street again.

'Investigators are supposed to get it wrong. Until they get it right. That's investigating. They rule some leads out. Then move on to the next lead, correct?'

'Ahh,' he says, shaking his head. 'It's hard to explain... I mean, I texted the girl, telling her I was right around the corner, Celina. That I was coming to get her. She thought I was only a couple of minutes away from saving her.'

'Oh, Len-ny,' Celina says. But that's all she says... allowing another silence to wash its way across the continent, from Lier in northern Belgium to Kobylisy in the heart of the Czech Republic.

'I mean, what have I ever achieved as an investigator?' Lenny fills in. 'Betsy? I hardly found her, did I? I was left a note telling me where she was. Benny Wilkinson? Eoghan Farrell. Deirdre Tully? They were all run-aways. I investigated over a hundred runaways. That's all. They were going to be found either way.

Whether I figured out they were hiding out in a friend of a friend's house first or not. I mean... how did I ever think I could work for the fuckin' PTU?'

'Language, Len-ny...' Celina says, the dimple on the edge of her lips creasing.

She was so surprised by Lenny's tongue when she first met him that she snapped 'Language Lenny!' to him in a serious tone, only for both of them to burst into laughter seconds into their stunned silence. The phrase has become a running joke between them ever since almost every time Lenny swears. Only Lenny isn't laughing this time. Instead, he blows out his cheeks, then washes a hand over the scalp of his shaved head.

'I'm an imposter. I'm no investigator.'

'Oh, Len-ny!' Celina says. 'Did you not figure out how to chat with this Sofie girl over Kindle?'

Lenny whistles a steady exhale, his eyes threatened with tears.

'Yes.'

'Well that is investigating, correct? Then what happened after you contacted her on Kindle?'

Lenny sighs.

'Well,' he says. 'I thought she was telling me that she was in the suspect's house. Ruthgar Bilic. But she wasn't. Cos I've just come out of that house, screaming her name like a fuckin' eejit!'

'Oh-kay,' Celina says, her accent thickening, her tone soft and sombre. And slow. And considered. Always considered. That's why Lenny learned to love Celina's company. Because of her considerate nature, there were frequent silences in her conversations. Just like the silence he was sitting in right now... But the silences were worth it. They were worth it to hear the truth. 'Aaaand... so, you can still text her on the Kindle, yes?' Celina asks.

'Yep,' Lenny says. 'Only I'm not chatting with her anymore. I'm chatting with a boy.'

'A boy, Len-ny? What you talking about?'

'Another boy. Who's also gone missing. And is being held with Sofie.'

'What, Len-ny?'

'Listen, this is why I'm calling, Celina... I wanna speak to the boys. And to you. I wanna speak to the three of you. Can you put the boys on... please?'

'Of course, Len-ny,' Celina says, her brow dipping, her eyes darting as she paces the kitchen of her cute cottage, to where double French doors open to a glistening green landscape that rolls away for miles until it meets the sky.

'Jar-red! Ja-kub!' she calls out.

With the flick of Celina's wrist, Lenny can see his sons' faces; their smiling faces—all teeth and gums.

'Hey, you two,' he shouts around the echoey, empty grey street of northern Prague.

'Daddy!' Jacob calls out, over the birds whistling in the background.

'Listen you three,' Lenny shouts, 'I'm sorry. I am. But I'm ringing to say I won't be home tonight. I've got a big job to do. So, I'll have to delay those hugs I promised you until tomorrow. You two okay with that?'

Lenny doesn't get a response, not verbally, but the grins on his sons' faces tell him all he needs to know. At the cottage, in the back garden of that cottage, around the rolling green fields that smother that cottage, Jared and Jacob have all they'll ever need.

'I love you!' Lenny shouts. 'But I gotta go. I gotta go do my job.'

He pokes a finger to the screen, ending the call before looking up and down the length of the empty grey street again, his bum numb from the pavement his bony ass collapsed to.

When he heaves himself back to his feet with the groan of an ageing man, he thumbs his phone again, taking him back to the Amazon Customer Services messages, noticing Liam has texted two more times while Lenny was taking a moment to wallow.

I don't know his name. But he has brown hair and a brown beard. And he drives a blue car.

'Awesome, kid,' Lenny whispers to the phone before scrolling to read the second message.

The house he lives in is small. Really small. It has a blue door. Number 78.

LIAM

I drop the Kindle to my lap, close my eyes and try to breathe in and out through my nose normally. As if everything is normal. When it's not normal. How can it be normal when I have been tied to this strange bed, in this strange house, by this strange man... Next to this strange girl? Sofie seems more scared than I am.

I read all of the messages she showed me on her Kindle from the private investigator Lenny Moon. That's how I know her name is Sofie. Now the private investigator's trying to find both of us. He got close to finding Sofie once. But I think he'll find us next time. Because I have been able to give him good clues. Better clues. Like, I told him I was taken in a blue car. And I told him I was, like, taken into a house with a blue door. And that the door had the number seventy-eight on it.

When I open my eyes again I am looking at Sofie. I can still see the old tears that rolled down her face earlier. Down one of her cheeks. But she's not crying new tears. She hasn't cried new tears since I got here. I want to hug her and tell her everything will be okay. That Lenny Moon is coming to save us. She must be seven or eight years of age. A year or two younger than me. Round about the same age as my little sister.

'Hmm, hmm,' she says, nodding at me. As if she is trying to tell me everything will be okay, too. And that she thinks like I think. That Lenny Moon is coming to save us.

She stretches her hand to my hand, and then my fingers wrap round hers. And when we are holding each other's fingers we hear a voice... Downstairs. The same voice that drove me here in that blue car. I thought he was being really nice, then he just kept driving and driving and driving... and when he told me he had a football to give to me that was signed by a famous footballer I was not sure if he was being really real. Like, properly real. When I walked into this bedroom and saw Sofie tied to the bed with Sellotape over her mouth, that's when I, like, knew he wasn't really for real. And now I'm tied to the bed beside her, with black Sellotape across my mouth.

'Hmm, hmm,' I say, nodding back at her. Just to let her know everything will be okay. That Lenny Moon is coming to save us. Then we can both go back to our families. And say sorry to them. Sorry that we were taken by the strange man with the dirty beard.

I wipe my cheek against my shoulder again. To catch another tear before Sofie sees me crying. And then the voice gets a little louder, as if he's right at the bottom of the stairs shouting up at us. If I could understand what he was saying I would be able to fully hear him. And then I would be able to text Lenny Moon some more clues. But I don't understand anything he's saying.

I start to think what other clues I can send Lenny Moon that will help him get here quicker. So, I tap at the screen of the Kindle, and I begin to type into the Amazon chat. Not a message for the private investigator. But one for Sofie to read.

We need to think of more clues to send to Lenny Moon

When I twist the screen to her, she stares into my eyes and nods and nods. Lots of nods.

'Hmm, hmm,' she says.

It's all she can say. It's all she or me can say.

I try to sit as tall as I can in the bed, pushing my bum to the rail just so I can, like, stare down at the carpet. But I can't see nothing. Just dirty, grey carpet. I look at the small radiator, then at the curtains pulled over the window. But they're just grey curtains. A bed and a carpet and some curtains in an empty room. That's all that's in here. I lean back up and look back at Sofie to see her nodding. She knows. She already knows there's no clues in this room. She must have looked around it herself with the light from the Kindle. I tap at the keyboard on the screen again and then I twist it back to her.

How long have you been here?

She looks at me as I pass her the Kindle, then she leans it on her belly and begins typing. Slowly. With one finger. It's not easy to type when your elbows are pinned to the bed rail.

I look up at the ceiling while she is typing. No clues there, either. Except whoever painted the wall grey touched the white ceiling with the paint brush a few times.

'Hmm, hmm,' she says, twisting the Kindle back to me.

I don't no I am no good with time

I look at her and I try to smile with my eyes, to let her know we will be okay. Then I take the Kindle from her to type in that 'everything will be okay,' when the Kindle screen gets lighter, and brighter, in my hands. And a new message from Lenny Moon pops into the inbox.

How many minutes do you think you were in the car for Liam?

I lean my head back on the rail, staring up at the bits of grey paint on the white ceiling that shouldn't be there, and I try to think... and think... It was only five minutes' walk from the hotel to the football training pitches. Because that is how I persuaded my mam and dad to let me go to football practice this morning. But we were definitely more than five minutes in the car, Because I started to get, like, worried in the car, long, long before we arrived at this horrible house. I begin typing. And then I show it to Sofie, as if she knows how long I was in the car for.

Between 10 and 15 minutes. I'm sure it was not longer than 15 minutes.

Sofie nods. And then I nod, because I think I am right. I was in the car for about the same time as Sofie thinks she was in the car for. About fifteen minutes. I'm sure I was...

I press at the arrow beside my message, and the text flies off to Lenny Moon. To wherever he is. Hopefully close by.

LENNY

14:40pm

Lenny stares down at the point of his leather shoes and shakes his head. Wrong shoes. Wrong day. If the PTU had have given any inkling that new recruits may indeed start work on the day of their actual interview, Lenny sure would have forgone the tight navy suit and expensive leather shoes he had been pacing and racing around in all morning. His battered New Balance trainers would have been ideal for the concrete jungle that is Prague. Concrete for miles and miles. Bright, white concrete that turns darker the further you travel away from the centre. Right now, his battered New Balance trainers were sitting on the back porch of Celina's cottage. Not far from where his two sons were grinning their wide smiles.

He glances at his phone and pinches at the screen, zooming in and out of row after row of the concrete jungle he is currently pacing. Grey street after grey street. Hundreds of them. Like a labyrinth web spraying in all directions.

He tuts, then slips his thumb upwards, clearing the webbed map from his screen and taps back into the Amazon Customer Service chat, reading back Liam's messages, to make sure he wasn't missing anything obvious. He wasn't. Blue car. Blue door. Number seventy-eight. That's what Liam had texted. All Lenny needs to do is find the number seventy-eight on this map of webbed streets that has a blue door. He clicks back into Google Maps with a rush wiggling through him where the cringing had been churning just moments ago, and swipes his way to the next street, searching for house number seventy-eight. To see if it has a blue door... Nope. A black door! He tries the next street... Finds seventy-eight. Another black door. Then the next street... A grey door...

He continues to swipe to the next street, zooming until he can find number seventy-eight, then he scratches at the stubble above his ear...

'Think Lenny,' he whispers, tutting again, scrolling his way back into the Amazon Chat, tip-tapping his thumbs against the keyboard.

How many minutes do you think you were in the car for Liam?

He sends his question off accompanied by the sound of a cool swoosh, then squints up at the grey street he is pacing down, making his way towards the maze of streets he has been scrutinising on Google Maps. He feels somewhat warmed in the knowledge that Sofie has a bigger boy beside her. A friend. Somebody to share her scare with.

His phone sizzles in his hand.

Between ten and fifteen minutes. I'm sure it was not longer than 15-minutes.

'Okay,' Lenny says, his pointed leather shoes screeching to a stop. 'So if Liam was taken from there...' He pinch-zooms at the screen to find The Grand Hotel Liam was walking back to when he was swiped, then he out-pinches the screen, stretching the map higher and higher, staring at the rows of streets that web away from the northern point of white-washed Prague. 'Okay, okay,' he repeats to himself. 'And if Sofie was taken from here and travelled for fifteen minutes in the car....'

Lenny squints at the screen as he zooms in and out... in... and then back out again, slower this time... until he claps his hands together, sandwiching the phone between them. 'Yes, man!' He shouts, high-fiving himself.

He palms the phone again, and spins his finger, circling a web of suburban Prague streets perhaps four miles in radius. Dozens of streets. Not hundreds. Hundreds of houses. Not thousands. His net is closing in, his imposter syndrome evaporating. If both children travelled north into the grey streets for fifteen minutes by car after they were swiped, then they must be in this radius. They *have* to be somewhere within this radius.

In his excitement, Lenny thumbs the phone, then presses it against the chest of his yellow puffer jacket, allowing the tone to pulse upwards.

'Lenny Moon,' she says, answering.

'Olette,' he says, as he sets off walking again.

'You want to take the Liam McLyn case, am I right?'

'Yes,' he says, his shoe suddenly stopping again. 'How did you know?'

'You got excited. Called to where you believed Sofie Le Saux was only to find she wasn't there...'

Lenny looks over both shoulders, as if a ghost is following him, then he walks on.

'What the fuck?' he says. 'How did you know that?'

'Happens,' she says. 'PIs on their first day, they can get over excited. That excitement dies down. Trust me. Besides, the Liam

McLyn case struck a chord with you, right? A family on holiday. An Irish family. An Irish boy.'

Lenny presses the phone firmer to the chest and tilts his head back so he can push an exhilarated exhale towards the sky.

'You're right, and you're wrong,' he says. Then he tilts his head back down, gripping the phone tighter. 'I did get overexcited. I thought I had Sofie in my sights. But I didn't….'

'Don't blame yourself,' Olette says.

'I'm not blaming myself,' Lenny says. 'Besides, that's only the part that you were right about. But I also said you were wrong...'

'Wrong about what?' Olette says.

'I'm not taking the Liam McLyn case because he's Irish. I'm taking it because I know where he is...'

Lenny's nostrils flare when he hears a scoff down the line.

'In the same way you knew where Sofie Le Saux was?' Olette asks.

'Kinda,' Lenny replies.

'Kinda?'

'Olette listen to me…. Sofie Le Saux and Liam McLyn were kidnapped by the same man who lives somewhere in the northern suburbs of Prague. North of Kobylisy.'

'Really?'

'Really!' Lenny spits, exhausted. 'I know because I've been communicating with both of them through Sofie's Kindle.'

There's a silence on the line... A hesitation.

'Are you for serious, Lenny Moon?'

'I sure fuckin' am,' he replies without hesitation. 'Look, I've narrowed my search to a four-mile radius. I'm right on the edge of that radius now, looking for a blue door, numbered seventy-eight.'

'Wait... what?'

'Liam McLyn was able to provide me that much information. Whoever swiped him, invited him into the house after picking him up in a blue car...'

'Wait... are you for serious Lenny Moon?'

'Olette, you gotta stop asking me am I for serious! And start listening... Listen to me good. Please. We need more PIs. We need numbers on these streets. I reckon there's about a hundred streets in my radius... We can close in on this guy... We can save Sofie and Liam in the next twenty minutes—'

'Wait. Hold on!' Olette says, before the line falls silent again. 'You're telling me,' she eventually says, 'that Sofie Le Saux and Liam McLyn are together? In a man's house? That they were both definitely swiped?'

'I am,' Lenny says. 'And I need a team. A team of PIs sent out to the suburbs north of Kobylisy.'

'A team?' Olette says. 'That's not how it works at the PTU. Yes, we have over two hundred PIs, but they're based all over Europe. They could be anywhere and everywhere right now.'

'We'll need to call the local police then, get their boots on the ground.'

'Yeah, uh,' Olette says, before pausing again. Hesitating. 'I'm impressed. We're impressed. You've done a great job, Lenny. I can't ever remember an investor cracking so much on his first day...'

'Thank you,' Lenny says, his uncomfortable pointed shoes swivelling into yet another grey street.

'Let me, uh...' Olette hesitates again. 'It's just the board have all left the offices. They carried out their interviews this morning, then spread the workload, now they're off doing... individual works.'

'Olette, we need to move. We need to move fast. As Dr Volgt said this morning, these children are sold as quickly as possible. The market moves fast and—'

'Lenny Moon,' Olette says, interrupting. 'I'm going to personally track Dr Volgt down for you and I'll get back to you as soon as I can. In fact, I'll have him ring you himself. You just keep making your way to the streets you think Sofie and Liam are being held in...'

'I'm on the edge of those streets now.... Please, Olette. Get him to call me as soon as you can...'

The phone pulses a dead tone, and Lenny exhales a deep sigh before taking it from his chest and scrolling through Google Maps again...

'Zdarska Street,' he whispers to himself as he walks... reading out loud the next street among the maze of grey streets he hasn't yet zoomed into... He pinches, then zooms, then pinches again... repeating his routine until suddenly he stops walking, his pointed shoes screeching to another halt. 'Holy shit. Number seventy-eight,' he says. 'It has a blue door!'

LIAM

I finish typing on the Kindle, and then I turn it to Sofie, watching her face light up with the brightness of the screen, and trying to see if under that black tape she is smiling. She sure is nodding.

If Lenny Moon knows I was 15 minutes in the car from where I was taken. And he knows you were 15 minutes in the car from where you were taken. Then he'll know exactly where we are. He'll save us, Sofie. He's coming. x

She looks up into my eyes after she is finished reading, and I nod. And then she nods. And then I stretch out my hand as far as the ropes will allow me to until I am putting my fingers inside hers again.

I'll look after her. I'll protect her. Just like I would protect Yvonne. My little sister. And then I remember that we were all supposed to go to the zoo today. And they'll all be angry with me.

Really angry. Mam. Dad. And Yvonne. I've ruined their holiday. Everybody's holiday. Just because I wanted to take part in football practice this morning.

Sofie squeezes my fingers tight with her fingers, and it makes me look up at her again. I think she knows I am getting sad. And mad. And feeling all sorts of horrible, horrible feelings. But I shouldn't be too sad. Or mad. I should be like Sofie's big brother. Looking out for her. Looking out for her and looking out for me. I will look after both of us until Lenny Moon comes and saves us. He will. I know he will. He will be narrowing down on the map exactly where we are now. Blue door. Number seventy-eight. Fifteen minutes from where I was taken from. And fifteen minutes from where Sofie was taken from. He won't be long.

His voice goes loud again downstairs. Talking. Talking on the phone. This is like the fifth phone call he has been on since he tied me to this bed. I wish I could speak Czech. Then I'd have so many more clues to text to Lenny Moon.

'Ctyri hodin,' I hear him say. Hodin. *Hodin*. I know that word. Dad said it like every day on our holiday. When booking restaurants. He would say 'sedm hodin'. Sedm means seven. Dad told me that. Which means hodin means o'clock. The man with the dirty beard keeps saying 'ctyri hodin'. Jedna, dva, tri, ctyri. Ctyri is four. Four o'clock.

I press my finger to see if there is a clock on the top of the Kindle. It's 3:02 now. He's going to do something with us in one hour. One more hour!

'Ctyri hodin.' I'm sure that's what he's been saying? Four o'clock? Or maybe I'm just guessing. Guessing what he is saying in a different language. I need to be more clear. I need to get things right before I text Lenny with any clues. I don't want to give him anything that will send him in, like, the wrong direction... So, I listen more to the phone call downstairs... to see if he says 'ctyri hodin' again... just so I can be sure.

I hear him say 'Ahoj', and I know that means both 'hello' and 'goodbye'—and then the talking ends. And me and Sofie kinda, like, look at each other and I nod at her. To let her know everything will be okay. That Lenny Moon is coming. That he knows where we are. And he's going to save us.

There's a creak outside, and Sofie's head turns to the door, then back towards me. Then another creak. I can hear him breathing as he walks up the stairs. I don't want to feel frightened. But I do. I feel really frightened. Really scared. Even though I know Lenny Moon is coming to save us. So, I throw the Kindle on to the bed between me and Sofie and then the bedroom door slaps open and there's light in the room. Then a man. A man with a dirty beard.

'Hmm, hmm,' is all I can hear myself shout. 'Hmmm!' Inside my own head.

He looks at me, then puts a finger up to his lips.

'Shhh,' he says.

He sits himself onto the bed beside Sofie.

'Hmmm!' I shout. Or try to shout, rocking the bed rail back and forward as much as I can.

'Quiet boy!' he says, turning to me. 'Or I will hurt you. And her.'

I stop rocking. And I swallow. And swallow again. Scared. Really scared. Then I lean my head back on the bed rail, my breathing all loud inside my ears and I watch him stand up, reach behind Sofie, and begin pulling and pulling at her...

SOFIE

I feel scared. So, so scared. Especially with him behind me. Breathing. Breathing hard. And loud. And warm. I can feel his breathing on the back of my ear. And in my hair. I just look at Liam. Until I feel my arm being tickled. My arm twisting. Backward and forward. Up and down. Until it's not tickling no more. It's hurting. Hurting bad. So, so bad. Until my arms fall free. And loose. And I can breathe better. So much better.

I lift my hands and look at them, twisting them round and around until I see Liam through my fingers. When I take my hands away I nod at him. Once. Then I shake my shoulders. Shake my arms. Because I haven't moved them in so, so long.

Suddenly, the man grabs me from behind, squeezing his arm against my belly, resting his chin on my shoulder. Breathing heavy in my ear.

'Stay quiet, yes?'

I nod again. And then I suck up my nose, so that I don't cry in front of Liam. And when the man grabs me tighter around my belly, he lifts me off the bed until I am standing on my feet, staring up at him, staring up at his ugly nose.

'Don't move!' he says.

I nod again. And then he kneels down and twists my body around. I look at Liam. He looks shocked. Scared. Probably just as scared as I am. My hands tickle. And I know it's the rope tickling them. It tickles before it hurts... Really hurts. He pulls the rope too tight around my wrists and I make a squeak sound.

'You okay?' the man with the beard says, standing back up.

'Hmm, hmm,' I say, nodding.

I don't know why I'm nodding when I should be shouting 'no'. How could I be okay? My hands are tied behind my back. I don't know you. I don't know where I am. I don't know why I'm here. I don't know why you've taken me... But maybe I was surprised because he wanted to know if I was okay. Nobody ever asks me if I am okay.

I look up at him even higher this time. Not just at his ugly nose. And when we look into each other's eyes I see a man. Not just a scary man with a beard. But a normal man with a beard. A man with a beard like any other man with a beard. But he doesn't look into my eyes for long. He looks away from me.

'It won't be long,' he whispers as he walks away.

And I nod back to nobody.

'Hmmm, hmmm,' I say.

What won't be long? *What won't be long?*

He continues walking. All the way to the other side of the bed. Where he sits. Right next to Liam's face.

'I do not want to hurt you. But I will,' he says. 'I will hurt you and her if you move when I untie your ropes.'

Liam doesn't say anything... until he nods.

I feel scared. So, so scared. Scared that Liam might try to run. And leave me. Leave me here all on my own again.

My breathing gets all loud inside my ears. Inside my own head. I haven't heard my breathing this loud since Liam came here and made me feel safer.

The man with the beard bends behind Liam and starts to

untie his ropes and I wonder when private investigator Lenny Moon will get here.

When Liam moves his arms, circling them up and down, I stare at him, hoping he doesn't run. But he doesn't... he just sits forward a little on the bed. Squeezing his arms backwards and forwards. Until the man with the beard leans over him.

'You try to run, I will hurt you. And her.' Liam looks at me while he nods and then suddenly the man rolls him onto his belly. 'Keep still!'

Liam keeps looking at me while he is lying flat on the bed, and as he is looking I shake my head. Don't run, Liam. He'll catch you. And hurt you. And hurt me, too. Or worse... you'll get away. And I'll be left here all on my own again.

He shakes his head back at me as his hands are being tied, as if he is hearing what I am saying inside my own head. Then, suddenly, the man with the beard pulls him up to his feet. And the two of us are standing now. On opposite sides of the bed. And I can see him. Really see him. See that he is just a boy, too. And he doesn't know what to do the same as I don't know what to do.

A tear falls from my eye. And suddenly it is dripping off the black tape and onto the carpet beside my foot, so I rub my eye into my shoulder before Liam sees me crying and that's when I see it. The Kindle. Private investigator Lenny Moon. Face down in the middle of the bed.

When I look back up, I see that Liam has been looking at me looking at the Kindle and I shake my head at him. He nods back to me. And now I'm confused. So, so confused. About everything. About everyone. About the man with the beard. About private investigator Lenny Moon. About Liam. I'm just confused. Confused and angry. Angry with myself for walking and walking away from the orphanage this morning.

'Tu es stupide, Sofie!' I say inside my own head.

'What did you say?' the man with the beard asks as he is tightening the ropes around Liam's hands.

'Hmm, hmm,' I say, shaking my head.

He stares at me, and I see the eyes that make him look like a normal man with a beard, and not just a scary man with a beard again and I don't feel scared anymore. I just feel more confused. More confused and more angry.

He stands up and starts to push at Liam's shoulder, walking him out of the bedroom. Into the light.

'Remember,' I hear him say, 'If you try to run, I will hurt you.... And her. Stay there.'

I hear his footsteps coming back. Back to me. And when I see his head, he flicks it and I walk towards him until he pushes the back of my shoulder, too, walking me towards Liam at the top of the stairs.

'The two of you together, go down. I will be right behind you. Front door is locked. So don't try anything.'

I look at Liam and swallow, but Liam has already started to walk down the first step without looking at me. So, I step down too and I remember when I was dragged up these steps this morning. Scared. More scared than I am now. Now I'm just confused. And angry. Angry with myself.

'Wait there,' he says when we reach the bottom.

He creeps in front of us and that's when Liam looks at me, and I shake my head at him. Telling him to not run. To not try anything.

The man with the beard opens the front door and peeks outside, before turning back to look at both of us.

'You,' he says pointing at me. 'You first. If you do as I say, and stay quiet, you will get a reward. Do you understand?'

I nod my head at him.

'Hmmm,' I say.

And I don't know why I'm nodding at him all of the time.

Agreeing with everything he says... When he puts his finger to his mouth.

'Shut up. No noise. Do you understand?'

I nod my head again. And then he walks over to me, pushes at my shoulder, and leads me out the front door, towards his car. I feel stupid for not remembering it was blue. I knew it was blue. I just couldn't remember for sure. I look up and down the street while I am outside. But I don't see anybody. Or anything. I don't see Lenny Moon.

The man with the beard pulls the car door open and I am thrown into the back seat.

'Remember,' he says, standing in the door while I am face down on the seat. 'Stay quiet. Keep your head down. If you do as I say, you will get a reward.'

He slams the door closed, and suddenly everything is even more quiet. As if I can just hear inside my own head. I know I am getting scared. As well as confused and angry. Scared that he is not bringing Liam with me. I want to look up. To see the front door of the house, to where Liam is. I hope he's not running. I hope he's coming with me. He better be coming with me...

LENNY

15:05pm

Lenny subtly rolls his index finger against the screen of his phone, squinting at the next street amongst the dwindling maze of streets within his narrowed four-mile radius before pinching to zoom in to find number seventy-eight on that street. He tuts when he notices the door is painted black. Like most of the doors around these northern suburbs.

Lenny has completed this same scroll-and-pinch routine on a hundred streets while he paced towards the only street within his four-mile radius where he found the number seventy-eight has a blue door. Zdarska Street. Four turns away. A right. Two lefts. And then one more right... About five minutes' walk at his current pace.

He glances up the vacant, grey street he is now pacing, then back to the phone, rolling his finger again against the screen, squinting at the next street amongst the dwindling maze of streets, then pinching in to find number seventy-eight... Only, this street doesn't have a number seventy-eight. Then he repeats his routine. Rolling his finger and pinching in...

He blows out his cheeks as he fingers his way through his routine, and after another glance back up to take the sharp right turn, he checks the time at the top of his phone. 3:06pm.

He blinks his eyes repeatedly, then swipes up and out of Google Maps before tapping into his call records: to see what time it was he last spoke with Olette.

2:50pm.

'Fuck sake,' he says. 'Sixteen minutes.'

He hovers his finger over the PTU's phone number and sighs before stabbing against it, allowing the tone to trill as he grips the phone under his chin... waiting... and waiting... as the tone chirps... and chirps... and chirps... before cutting out, then throbbing.

'Oh, come on!' he shouts, his frustration echoing back to him.

He huffs and puffs, then logs back into Google Maps, checking first that he is on the right path to Zdarska Street, following the orange line that is leading him to the only blue door numbered seventy-eight that he has so far found, noticing he'll arrive at his destination in just four minutes. In four minutes, he might have rescued Sofie Le Saux and Liam McLyn in one swoop. But he's trying to not get as excited as he was when he was approaching Ruthgar Bilic's house an hour ago.

He brushes a finger up the screen and gets back to searching the final maze of streets he hasn't yet searched within his narrowed radius; checking for number seventy-eight on the next row, only to find there is no seventy-eight on that row. And that there likely won't be any seventy-eights on the rows after that either, for they run the same length as this one. He scrolls up and down subtly, shaking the screen, searching for longer streets, then clicking into them, then scrolling. He finds a number seventy-eight, then zooms in to see another black door. Most doors are black. Or grey. To match everything else around here.

Then he scrolls again to repeat the process, glancing up every few strides to make sure he's following his route. Just three more turns to Zdarksa Street... Three more minutes...

He glances down, rolls his finger against the screen, and continues the routine, zooming in, shaking his head, then zooming out to find the next street of appropriate length... Before trying again... and again... and again. Until his pointed shoes screech to a stop against the pavement. Number seventy-eight. With a blue door. Vetrna Street. One point two miles away from where he is now. In the most northern point of the radius he had narrowed his search to. The second blue door he has found within that entire radius that is numbered seventy-eight. A warmth wiggles its way around his stomach, and he shivers on the spot, before turning another corner onto another grey street just as the phone begins to sizzle in his hand.

'Olette,' he says, answering 'What the heck? You've missed my last two calls...'

'Lenny I'm trying to get hold of Dr Volgt for you. He's uh... he's still at lunch.'

'Lunch?'

'He doesn't like to be bothered at lunch. None of the board do. They see food as their respite. Lunch and dinner is the only time they're off the clock. We've had an assistant go chase them, though. They're always in one of two restaurants in the city...'

'Wait... what?' Lenny says, his bald head shaking.

'Lenny, you've done an incredible job. This doesn't happen to every new PI. Not on their first day. Rarely ever on any day to be honest. Every case is unique, but this sure is something... Which is why we need the board's say on this.'

'O-kay,' Lenny says, his head still shaking. 'We just need feet on the streets, Olette. That's all. We need numbers on the ground. To check doors marked seventy-eight within a few small suburbs of northern Prague...'

'Lenny, we will be with you as soon as we can...'

'Well, now would be as soon as you can, Olette!' Lenny snaps, before holding his eyes closed. 'I'm sorry. Look, Olette, I've narrowed it down. I think Sofie Le Saux and Liam McLyn may well be in one of two possible houses...'

There's a silence on the line. Not a hesitation. A silent shock... Until Olette kisses her lips.

'Lenny, you'll learn this. But the PTU is not like the police force. We don't have units. And units within units... We have individuals chasing individual cases. Right now, one of the assistants in the office is chasing Dr Volgt down. It won't be long. We'll have a decision on your investigation soon. Real soon, Lenny. Within minutes. I promise.'

'Olette, look, let's just call the police. We'll have all those streets checked within the next quarter of an hour. In quarter of an hour we will have saved two swiped children.'

'We're minutes from tracking down Dr Volgt, and then you'll know what the PTU's action is, Lenny. You're still minutes away from finding these children either way, right? If they are where you say they are, Lenny. You'll get them. You'll save them. You say you've narrowed it to two possible houses?'

'I'm on the edge of one of the two blue doors now. One more turn away...'

'You are?' Olette says.

'Yep. The next blue door after that is one point two miles away. A twenty-minute walk for me. Less if I run. I'm saving these children within the next quarter of an hour anyway... But Olette, get bodies to seventy-eight Zdarska Street and seventy-eight Vetrna Street as soon as possible.'

'We will. I promise,' Olette says.

'What the hell is going on up there in the PTU?' Lenny says in one breath, the words projectiling from within him.

'Uh, Lenny, if only you knew...' Olette says with a sigh. 'Look, you've made an incredible breakthrough, and we thank you. We do. I promise you, Lenny, we'll have feet on the street for you soon... As soon as I get Dr Volgt's decision. I'll ring you back. Soon as I can.'

Lenny sighs into the phone, a deep sigh that makes it all the way to the penthouse suite of The Empire Tower—the highest point in all of Prague. Then the dead tone throbs from his screen, just as he is pivoting around his final turn.

As he pockets his iPhone into his yellow-puffer jacket, he stares at the cracked concrete road on the battered metal sign hanging on the far grey wall.

Zdarska Street.

He quickens his pace, pivoting his bald head left, then right.

'That side,' he says to himself, crossing the street. He holds his breath. Excited. Exhilarated. Exhausted. That sure was a lot of walking.

'These fucking shoes,' he says as he passes door number seventy-four... then seventy-six... his breathing now panting, his mind sprinting, his eyes blinking. Seventy-eight. Seventy-eight Zdarska Street. A blue door. A blue door that he leans an ear towards, listening... Listening before curling his knuckles into a ball and rattling them against the wood.

A rumble from inside. A rumble on the stairs. Up the stairs. Like a tud. Followed by another tud. Then a whizzing noise... Like a zipline. A fucking zipline?

Lenny leans back, sucks a deep inhale to his lungs and holds it there, his eyebrows knitting before he leans his ear to the door again... To hear a sigh. A definite sigh. A heavy sigh. The sigh of somebody not happy. Not happy they have to answer the door. Then footsteps... getting closer, and closer... Until the blue door creaks open, and a tiny elderly woman with tight, curly white hair squelches her nubbed nose at him, staring at his yellow-puffer jacket at first, then up into his pale, confused face.

'Sorry, ma'am,' Lenny says, almost bowing his head, noticing an electric stairs-chair over the woman's hunched shoulder. 'I, uh... knocked on the wrong door.'

He spins the heels of his pointed leather shoes on her doorstep, and stares at his phone, squinting at the map in front of him, tapping his thumb against the only other street he found inside his radius in which the number seventy-eight has a blue door. Vetrna Street.

'Twenty-two minutes' walk,' he whispers, 'ten if I run.'

He starts his sprint from a standing position, his leather shoes slap-slapping against the cracked concrete, the arms of his yellow puffer jacket whizzing either side of him...

LIAM

The car smells. Really bad. Like vomit. Like that time Yvonne vomited on the carpet upstairs at home. And I nearly vomited on the carpet upstairs from the smell of her vomit on the carpet upstairs. Until I ran out of the house. But I can't run away from this smell... Me and Sofie are stuck with it.

I can tell she is scared. She's not, like, crying, or making any noises. But I know she is scared because her body is still. And stiff. Stiff like a board. Scared stiff lying alongside me in the back seat, her face where my feet are. Her feet where my face is.

I think I want to cry. But I don't want to be the first to cry. Not if I am supposed to be Sofie's big brother. I'll only cry if she cries. But I'm afraid to bend down to look at her face, because he might hurt me if I move, even though he's not in the car. Not yet anyway. He threw me in the back seat next to Sofie, then told us to keep our heads down or he will hurt us, then he slammed the door shut and the car doors locked. And then, nothing... nothing has happened since. But I'm not looking up to see if he is outside. I'm not moving at all. I'm as stiff as Sofie is lying on this backseat. Scared stiff.

The ropes are tight on my wrists. Tighter than my arms were

tied to the bed. I can move my hands in circles, round, and round. I just can't free them. Not yet anyway. But I am trying. Trying to turn my wrists in circles, hoping the ropes get looser and looser.

A cry almost bursts through my nose. But I suck it up and then I try to keep silent, to see if I can hear Sofie crying. But she's still just stiff as a board. As quiet as a mouse.

I try to reach my fingers towards her, just to touch her. And I feel her back, just below her shoulder... So I stretch my fingers further down and that's when her fingers grab on to mine. Tightly. Her fingers are cold. Really cold. But it's nice. It's nice for us to hold fingers again. And we both feel less stiff.

As we are holding fingers, we hear footsteps... getting closer... Then the back door snatches open, and Sofie lets my fingers go...

'Here,' the man with the dirty beard says, 'I told you I'd give you a reward.'

There's a slap on the seat beside us, then something crashes to the footwell. And when it lands I can see it. Facedown. The Kindle. He went back to get the Kindle for Sofie. Her reward for staying quiet.

When he shuts the back door, Sofie's body shuffles around until he opens the front door and sits into the driver's seat. Then she goes all stiff again. And I breathe in the horrible vomit smell as I lean my head down more and more, crunching my chin into my neck... When Sofie twists a little, I can see her... I can see her face. Her eyes. Her sad eyes.

She blinks at me. And I breathe in through my nose before blinking back at her. And then she nods her head. And I nod my head before she nods towards the footwell, towards the Kindle lying on the floor of the car. I twist around and stare at it again, then back down at her before shrugging my shoulder. I don't know, Sofie. I don't know what to do... What I can do... Our hands are tied behind our backs. We can't reach the Kindle. And even if we could, we can't type on it. We can't give Lenny Moon any more clues about where we are. Not with our hands tied behind our backs.

A tear falls down the side of my face. Then another tear. So, I wipe the side of my cheek into the dirty, smelly seat that stinks of vomit and now half of my face probably stinks of vomit, too.

He makes a horrible noise with the gear stick, like a crunch and a click, then the car pulls off, slowly at first, before he quickens up and his indicators begin to tick-tock, tick-tock. I hate that noise. So, I squeeze my eyes shut, and when I open them, I see that Sofie is staring at me.

But I don't know what to do... So, I just shrug my shoulders at her. I don't know what I can do, Sofie... I'm sorry, But I don't...

Then I hear it again. The tick-tocking. The horrible indicator noise. We're turning another corner... Getting further and further away from the blue door with number seventy-eight on it. And now Lenny Moon will never find us. And the tears start coming. Fast. From both eyes. Then faster, rolling down my cheeks and onto the smelly seat. I feel Sofie's fingers, against my leg, then moving up to my back so she can pinch my fingers again...

LENNY

15:24pm

Lenny screeches his pointed leather shoes to a stop after skidding around the final corner, then he pauses momentarily to read, with his breaths heavy and panting, the battered sign nailed to the concrete wall.

Vetrna Street

The only other street in the four-mile radius Lenny had narrowed his search to on which the number seventy-eight's front door is blue.

He bends over, gripping his knees, and sucks in heavy breaths.

'These fuckin' shoes,' he groans, stretching down to wrap his fingers around his ankles, squeezing the discomfort away.

When he catches his breath, he stands back upright and looks up Vetrna Street, pivoting his head left and right, until he realises he is on the right side of the pavement already.

He almost walks by it in his haste. It was only three houses in. The blue door with the number seventy-eight nailed to it. After staring at the number, Lenny looks down to take in the concrete step beneath the door, noticing a leaf miraculously growing through one of its cracks.

'Holy fuckin shit!' he whispers to the step before his head darts upwards. 'This is the house... this is it!'

He takes a step back and stares at the tiny, grey terraced home. Three windows. Two upstairs. One downstairs, next to the faded blue door.

Then he steps forward again and leans his ear towards that door... to hear nothing but silence. A deathly silence. He curls his knuckles into a ball, then rattles them against the door, his knock echoing the length of the grey street.

'Hello!' he calls out. 'Ahoj. Ahoj.'

He knocks again. Thumping the door harder with the side of his fist.

'Ahoj!'

After pausing for hint of a reply, Lenny stands back and stares the tiny house up and down again, his eyes darting before they begin to blink, as they usually do when he is thinking... thinking things through. The lane ways. At the back of the houses!

Lenny paces back the way he came, then across the house on the corner towards the narrow gap behind it that leads to the rear of the grey houses on Vetrna Street. He points a finger at the roofs as he counts down three, until he reaches the back of number seventy-eight. And when he stretches to his tip-toes to stare over the grey wall, he can see that the house looks much the same from the back as it does from the front. Three windows. Two upstairs. One downstairs. Next to an unloved door.

He runs his fingers across the top of the grey wall, as if looking for a clue, then he inhales and exhales sharply before pushing his forearms to the top, heaving himself upwards, his yellow-puffer jacket scuffing as he climbs. When he sits atop the wall, he stares down at the concrete back yard in front of him, no bigger than the table he and his boys have been eating breakfast at since they emigrated to Belgium a little over three weeks ago.

When he drops from the wall — his pointed leather shoes slapping to the concrete in front of the narrow grey back door — he leans his ear towards the door... Another dead silence.

'Ahoj,' he says, banging his knuckles against the door. 'Ahoj. Sofie! Liam!'

He pushes at the door to find it locked. But not securely. The top and bottom of the door can open by about two inches when pushed, but the centre of it is held by a bolt. He pushes at the door again. Then harder. Rattling it.

'Ahoj!'

He takes a step back, to stare the rear of the ugly grey house up and down again. Then he steps towards the door and pushes hard with one hand, jiggling it a little before pushing it with two hands, pushing harder... and harder, before shouldering it... then shouldering it again... harder... until the bolt snaps open, and the door flings back, slapping against the side of kitchen cupboards.

He stands in the narrow concrete back yard, momentarily stunned, staring into the darkness of the kitchen before tentatively stepping one of his pointed leather shoes inside.

'Ahoj!' he calls out.

He walks further into the grey kitchen to be met by more greyness; grey cupboards, grey Lino on the floor; grey tiles on the walls. No kettle. No microwave. No appliances at all. A gap in the kitchen space where the washing machine should be.

'Ahoj!'

His own voice echoes hauntingly back to him.

'Ahoj!'

He walks through the tiny, vacant grey kitchen, then down the narrow hallway from where he pokes his head into a mostly vacant sitting-room save for an old, battered sofa, and a box TV screen sitting on the carpet—a cable hanging loose from the back of it. The house looks empty. As if nobody lives here. Not anymore.

'Ahoj!' he tries once more, before spinning on the spot and strolling out to the narrow hallway from where he places his foot onto the first step of a pokey, narrow flight of stairs that lead to the dark hole above him.

'Sofie! Liam!'

His voice echoes back from the hole, and he holds his eyes closed, frustrated. Scared.

'Fuck!' He flicks the word from his bottom lip as the step beneath his foot creaks under his weight. Then he walks up the rest of the steps slowly, and when he reaches the top he glances inside a small bathroom before stepping into a larger bedroom, to see a ruffled cream sheet on a makeshift double bed. It's pillow worn. Somebody does live here. Or used to live here.

'Ahoj!'

He walks back out onto the landing, facing the door that leads to the back bedroom, and as soon as he pushes it open he can smell them. He can smell the fright of Sofie and Liam. And when he steps towards the bed rail he knows for sure he's in the right place. Wrong time. But the right place.

'Holy fucking shit,' he says, fingering the remnants of the ropes that had been tying Sofie and Liam to the bed. 'Holy fucking shit!'

He spins, his mind racing, his gut rotating.

'Sofie! Liam!'

He roars their names. But all he can hear is his own voice reverberating through the vacant house. He drops to his knees, then falls flat to his stomach so he can squint under the bed. Nothing... Nothing but dust and fluff.

'Holy fucking shit,' he whispers to himself as he pushes and steps back to his feet.

He shovels his hand into the deep pocket of his yellow jacket and retrieves his phone, disappointed to see there have been no new messages from Liam or Sofie.

His thumbs begin to rapidly stab at the screen, typing a message to them...

I'm here. I'm in the house you were taken to. But I was too late. Where are you? Can you text me any clues as to where he has taken you?

Lenny holds his eyes closed as his message sends off accompanied by the sound of a cool swoosh, before spinning his pointed shoes on the spot and pacing down the narrow landing, entering the bigger bedroom at the front of the house. He drops to his knees again, then flat to his stomach to look under the bed. Cobwebs... Balls of fluff... The whole house seems empty but for the battered sofa downstairs, and the unplugged box television. Whoever kidnapped Sofie Le Saux and Liam McLyn sure doesn't intend on returning here. That seems certain. This house is dilapidated. It's not a home. Not anymore.

Lenny opens the drawers next to the double bed. One book. With a title he cannot read because consonants are difficult to pronounce in Czech. As he flicks through the book, a marker falls out and when it lands on the dirty carpet beside his pointed leather shoes, he sees that it is a stream of photos. A stream of passport photos. Three of them. Of a middle-aged man, with a dirty brown beard and matted brown hair.

'You mother fucker,' Lenny whispers to the photos. 'You dirty mother fucker!'

He pockets the photos, then stabs his thumbs to the screen of his phone again, logging into his call history and pressing his finger against the last number he had dialled. The tone echoes through the empty house, throbbing next to his ear... until it cuts out. Nobody at the PTU is answering. Again.

'I can't believe this,' he says, staring around the greyness of the bedroom before walking out to the narrow landing and eventually shuffling his way down the stairs, chicaning into the vacant sitting-room. He runs his hand over the sofa before turning to the TV where he fingers the cable hanging loose from a socket at the back.

'Iko Cable,' he whispers to himself, reading the sticker wrapped around the wire.

He thumbs his phone again, then stabs a finger at it before lifting it back to his ear.

'Ahoj, Iko Cable,' a voice says. 'Mohu Pomoci?'

'English. I need somebody who speaks English...'

'English, yes Sir. I speak English. This is Iko Cable. How can I help you?'

'I, uh... I live at seventy-eight Vetrna Street... can you bring up my account?'

'Of course, Sir...Just one moment.'

LIAM

The tick-tock, tick-tocking of the indicator is making me more mad than anything. More mad than the smell is making me feel. More mad than having my hands tied behind my back. The sound is just going through my ears and my brain... Tick-tock... tick-tock...

I wipe the side of my face into the horrible, stinky car seat again, and when I open my eyes and bend my neck down, Sofie is staring up at me.

She nods towards the footwell again, and I twist around really quietly to stare down at the Kindle. I'm not sure what she wants me to do. What I can do...

I roll over even more, as silently as I can, and then I press my feet to the door of the car, pushing myself a bit taller along the back seat. I try to stretch my hands downwards, even though there's no point. Even if I could reach the Kindle, I wouldn't be able to text. Neither will Sofie.

So, I roll back over on my belly quietly, and I shrug my shoulders at Sofie, just as he starts talking on the phone. Again. There's nothing I can do, Sofie. I'm sorry. But my hands are tied just like yours are tied...

When Sofie looks away from me, I listen to him talking with my cheek pressed to the smelly back seat. Talking and talking... In Czech. Just Czech. No English. I try to listen for English words... or any words I might know. But I can't understand anything he is saying. Not one word.

As he's talking, he flicks the indicator again, and the tick-tock, tick-tocking makes me want to just go all crazy. To scream. And, like, squirm. And kick. Kick at the doors. Kick at the windows. Kick at his head. Kick at that indicator, breaking it in two.

I start to turn my hands in circles instead, really angry, circle after circle, round and round and round. But it's not doing any good. It's just burning me, burning my wrists. My left wrist especially. It's sore. Really sore. So, I stop circling my hands. And I feel as if I need to cry again. As if I need to keep crying until he takes us out of this horrible, smelly car and unties our wrists. Then Sofie can get her Kindle back to read. And we can find out how close Lenny Moon is to saving us.

I close my eyes with my cheek still pressed to the smelly back seat and I think of my mam and my dad. And how angry they are going to be. How angry they must be right now. I bet Yvonne is crying. Crying because we didn't go to the zoo. Crying because her big brother ruined the family holiday. All because he wanted to do some football practice in the morning. I wonder if Sofie is thinking the same. That her mam and dad will be really angry with her for not coming home. And I begin to wonder if she has a sister like me? Or two sisters? Or maybe a brother? I wonder what it's like to have a brother. And then I try to think about my cousins who are boys, imagining they were my brothers, because I want to think about anything but being in this smelly car.

I suck up through my nose really hard to stop myself from crying. To stop myself from getting angry. And to stop myself from thinking about trying to not think about being in this car. Then I look down at Sofie again and I see that she has her eyes closed. She's probably trying to do what I'm trying to do. Think. Think about anything. Anything but being here right now. Lying down in the back of this smelly car, her hands tied behind her back. And Sellotape across her mouth.

I can't do this! I can't do this! I twist and twist, and circle and circle my wrists. Round and round. Round and round. Stretching them to the left. Then to the right. My left wrist hurts most. Like it's burning. So, I keep that hand still, and I roll, and twist, and circle my right wrist on its own. Over and over again. It's definitely loose. Looser than my left wrist. It's not burning as much when I twist it. Not yet... So, I keep twisting and twisting... circling and circling, stretching the rope, then rolling round... and round... until it hurts too much that I have to stop. My two wrists are, like, burning now, properly burning, and I breathe in and out really slowly through my nose, before swallowing and nodding to myself. Because I think I can do this! I think I can get my right hand free. I just need time. I need time to let the burning go away. Then I can start twisting and circling round and round again. My right hand will come loose. It's already come a bit loose. The rope has gone past my wrist now. It's halfway up my hand.

I listen to him on the phone while I wait on the burning pain to go away, trying to hear any English words. Any words I might understand. I've heard him saying 'ano' a few times which means 'yes'. But that's not much help. Everybody says 'yes' lots of times. Hundreds of times every day. Maybe even thousands of times every day. That's no clue.

Then the tick-tocking goes on again. And I want to free my right hand so bad, so I can break that small indicator stick from underneath the steering wheel.

I stretch and bend my fingers. As far as I can. To try to get rid of the pain in my wrists. Then, I close my fist into a ball, and I start again, rolling my right wrist, circling it, stretching it, and stretching it, then rolling again until half of my hand slips through, and now I feel I can definitely do it. I can definitely get my right hand free. I twist and twist, then circle and circle, before pulling really hard, when suddenly the rope stretches and my thumb slips through first, then the whole of my hand.

I duck my head down to stare at Sofie and she looks at me as if she is waiting on me to nod. Because I always nod at her when we see each other's eyes. But I don't nod this time. Instead, I take my hand from behind my back really slowly and quietly, and I show it to her. Her eyes go wide, and while the indicator is still tick-tocking and he's still talking really fast on the phone, I roll over a little on the backseat and drop my hand to the footwell, feeling the mat at first, then the cold steel of the Kindle.

LENNY

15.20pm

Lenny holds his eyes closed before whistling a slow, soft, satisfied exhale through his thin lips.

'Thank you, Sir,' he says. 'You've been most helpful.'

'No. Thank you, Mr Horata for being a customer of Iko Cable. Maybe you will be a customer of Iko Cable again someday.'

'Maybe,' Lenny says, before stabbing a finger to the phone, ending the call.

Without hesitating he clicks into the Amazon Customer Service chat again. No reply. Not since 14:44pm.

'Thirty-six fuckin' minutes ago,' he says, dropping the phone back into the pocket of his jacket and turning into the deathly silence of the house. When, somewhere in the distance there is a promise of sound... Purring at first. Then wailing. Louder... and louder. Wheels can be heard screeching over the siren. Not that far from the lonely, vacant house Lenny was now stood in. The siren screams, echoing outside, and then tyres screech to a halt, causing Lenny to race to the blue front door, snatching it open. To see two black BMWs with flashing blue lights on their roofs parked diagonally across Vetrna Street, their tyres steaming. He nods at the smartly-dressed man stomping out of the first car, before his brow begins to dip as that man sprints towards him.

'No, no, no,' a woman calls. A familiar voice. A voice Lenny has heard too many times already today. 'Leave him. He's with us. That's our guy.'

'Olette,' Lenny says, squinting at the rolled-down front window of the second BMW. 'What the fuck? I've been trying to... trying to call.'

'I told you we'd be here,' Olette says, as she pushes the door open and steps out. 'Well?'

She leans her back against the door of the BMW.

'Well, what?' Lenny says.

'Is this the address?'

'It is,' he says, nodding. 'But we were too late. Minutes too late. There's evidence in the back bedroom. Ropes. Ropes that were used to tie Sofie and Liam to the bed post. They're gone.'

'How do you know they were tied to a bed post, Moon?' a gruff voice grunts.

Lenny squints, beyond the smartly-dressed man standing in front of him to the side of Olette, to see bushy eyebrows like upside down Nike logos hovering above beady eyes, glaring through the gap of the wound-down back window.

Lenny steps off the concrete step.

'I, uh... I know they were tied by ropes to a bedpost because Sofie and Liam told me themselves. Through the Amazon Customer Service chat on the Kindle...'

As Lenny steps closer to the second BMW, the bloated face of Dr Volgt becomes clearer, his chin rounded and nodding, his cheeks wobbling.

'Good work, Moon. Good work.'

'Not good enough though, is it?' Lenny says, shrugging. 'We were too late. I told you,' he says, darting his stare at Olette. 'I told you over the phone we needed feet on the ground. That we needed to be quick.'

'We were quick,' Olette replies. 'Didn't you hear us?'

Lenny puffs out his cheeks as Dr Volgt snatches the back door of the second BMW open, heaving his large frame from the back seat and relieving the tyres of their pressure. He shuffles forward, then slaps Lenny where his bicep should be.

'Don't be hard on yourself, Moon, you did a good job.'

'I'm not being hard on myself,' Lenny snarls through his teeth, 'I'm being hard on you. On you, too,' he says, nodding at Olette. 'I knew they were here. I told you twenty minutes ago they were in one of two houses...'

'Lenny,' Olette says, tilting her head, 'We are here. We got here as quick as we could.'

'It's just...' Lenny doesn't finish his sentence. He can't finish his sentence... Instead, he nods.

'Josep,' Dr Volgt calls to the smartly-dressed man still standing in the doorway. 'Prohledejte dum!'

Lenny looks around to see the smartly-dressed man walking through the blue door.

'The back bedroom!' he shouts after him.

And when he turns back around as exasperated as he is exhausted, Dr Volgt slaps Lenny on the side of the arm again.

'Don't be upset, Moon. You look like someone pissed in your coffee. You've done a good job. Really good. Impressive investigating. But our main men will take it from here...'

Lenny looks at Dr Volgt, his nose stiffening, his eyes blinking.

'What's going on?' he says.

'We're here to take up your investigation...'

'No, I don't mean here, literally here,' Lenny says. 'I mean in general. What is going on with the PTU in general? Hiring a dozen investigators every day? One page of notes for those investigators to go on? Nobody answering my calls?'

Dr Volgt leans his bloated face closer to Lenny, one of his Nike-shaped eyebrows raising.

'Did I, or did I not, inform you this morning, Moon, that your job is to ask questions on the streets. Not inside the PTU. If you keep investigating like you have done this morning, you will end up a proud member of our unit. But if you keep asking questions of us and how we operate, you'll end up like most of our PIs. Out of a job within months.'

Lenny looks to Olette's marble eyes, trying to decipher if they are as perplexed by the PTU protocol as he is. But they blink away from him, and then she thins her lips. Lips that are clearly refusing to speak.

'Moon, your job is to investigate missing persons possibly involved in trafficking,' Dr Volgt continues. 'Not to antagonise the one unit set up to investigate these cases. Our senior men will take up your investigation. They may well get to the bottom of this before those two children are sold on. Josep will be contacting our forensics teams now. We'll work out who lived here as soon as we can. We'll know who swiped these children within the next hour. I wanna see this guy's ugly face. And I want the PTU to get that ugly face in for questioning.'

Lenny digs his hand into the deep pocket of his yellow jacket.

'This is his ugly face,' he says, pulling out the stream of passport photos. 'I found these in a book in the front bedroom. It's literally all that's in that house. This guy,' Lenny says, stabbing at the photos, 'isn't coming back here. The house has been cleared. He's gone.'

Dr Volgt coughs into the back of his hand, then looks up from the passport photos, darting his beady eyes between Lenny and then Olette.

'Good... good work, Moon. Maybe you will last in this unit

after all, huh? We'll take it from here. We'll get a name to this face and we'll track this bastard down.'

'His name is Horata. Javi Horata. I found that out by calling the TV cable company he had been using...'

'Javi Horata, huh?' Volgt says, nodding, wobbling his bloated cheeks. 'And you're sure this is our guy, Moon?'

'I'm certain,' Lenny says.

His jacket pocket vibrates while he is eyeballing Dr Volgt, and Lenny pops the studded button on it before diving his hand inside to grab for his phone.

'Holy fuckin' shit,' he says, staring at the screen. 'They've replied. Liam has replied. They're in the back of Horata's car right now...'

'That the Amazon Customer Service chat?' Olette says, stepping between Lenny and Dr Volgt.

'It is...' Lenny replies. 'I need.... I need one of these cars. I gotta... I gotta go get them.'

Dr Volgt coughs into the back of his hand again, then glances back over his shoulder at the black BMW he had sped to seventy-eight Vetrna Street in.

'Take this one, Moon,' he barks, 'Olette, you go with him!'

LIAM

I want to show Sofie the messages Lenny Moon has sent since I picked the Kindle up from the floor of the car. To let her know that he is in the house we were taken to. And that he is right behind us. Following us. Close to saving us. But I can't. I can't lift the Kindle up and turn it around to show her. He might turn around. And catch me. I need to leave the Kindle blocked from him, in front of my belly. So, instead, I keep blinking and blinking and nodding my head at Sofie, to let her know everything is going to be okay. That Lenny Moon isn't far behind us.

I think she knows what I am trying to say. I hope she does...

I read the message I just sent to Lenny Moon again. Telling him we are in the back of a car. A blue car. Over and over again... Waiting on him to message back. Telling me he's right behind us. Maybe I need to give him another clue. A clue to where we are. Because we could be driving anywhere.

But I would have to press my body up, to look out the window. And I don't think I can do that. Not without him seeing me. Or catching me. So, I press my cheek to the smelly seat again, with my hand over the screen of the Kindle and I wait on a new message box to light up.

The sound has changed. The sound of the car. The road it's driving on is different. It sounds more like home. Like the countryside. Like the sound the tyres make over the smooth roads in the Cork countryside. And there's no other sounds... No other cars. No indicators. No people. It's quiet. Really quiet. Except for the sound of the tyres, whizzing along the smooth road.

Then there's a buzz, and then a ring tone. Then his voice. Talking again. That's his fourth phone call now. He talks on the phone more than my mam talks on the phone. And then I think, and I wonder if he is talking to, like, the people he's taking us to. He's taking us somewhere. To someone. And that makes me lift my cheek from the seat and, slowly, I twist my neck a little to try to listen. But I can't hear anything. Or understand anything. He talks too fast. If he was speaking English that fast I probably still wouldn't know what he was saying. So, I twist back around quietly and look down at the Kindle again. No new message from Lenny Moon. Not yet anyway. I bow down further to see that Sofie is staring at me, her eyes wide open. I just nod again, lots of times. And I blink. To let her know Lenny Moon is right behind us. And then I wonder if I am lying to Sofie. Or even lying to myself. Lenny Moon might not be behind us. The last place he knew we were taken to was the house. He has no idea where we are now. And I have no clue to give him, except that we are in a smelly blue car. And that the roads are quiet. There's not much traffic. No noises at all actually. Just the car tyres driving fast over a smooth road. Like the roads my dad drives on back home.

I hold my eyes closed again and I suck in a big breath through my nose and hold it before rolling over a little, looking back over my shoulder at him. He has one hand on the steering wheel, the other hand holding the phone to his ear. Talking. And talking. Words I don't understand. Lots of words I don't understand.

So, I do it.... I don't even think about it. I just decide I'm doing it. I roll back over, and I press my hand to the seat, doing a press-up, getting higher, and higher... I see yellow out the window. Yellow grass. As far as I can see. Then I collapse back down to the smelly seat, pressing my cheek against it and breathing hard in and out of my nose as quietly as I can. I glance down at Sofie. Her eyes are really wide this time. Wider than before.

I blink at her, then nod. Before I roll over quietly again, noticing he is in the exact same position, the phone stuck to his ear, talking. And talking.

I roll back, then press my hand to the seat again and rise... and rise. Yellow. Yellow fields. Lots and lots of fields...

My chest collapses to the smelly seat again, and then my breaths get really quick and loud inside my head. That's a clue! That's a really good clue!

I stab my finger to the Kindle to touch the keyboard, and then I start typing...

We are driving on roads in lots of yellow fields. Yellow fields as far as I can see.

I smile inside the black tape. Because I got a good clue. If Lenny Moon knows how long ago it was we were taken from the house he'll know how far into the yellow fields we are. He's coming. I can feel it. He's coming. Lenny will be right behind us.

I look down at Sofie, and I nod my head lots of times. Lots and lots of times. Then I blink, and blink again. He's coming, Sofie. He's coming! I just got another clue!

I hold the Kindle close to my belly, waiting for a message to blink onto it from Lenny Moon, and then I press my cheek to the smelly seat again, trying to listen to the tyres over his voice talking and talking... Talking fast. In Czech. I think he's getting louder. As if he's getting angry. I don't want him to get angry. Not before Lenny Moon gets here to save us... Then he calms down... His voice gets lower. Wait... he just said 'hodin' again. 'Ctyri hodin'. He did. He definitely did. Four o'clock. I thought I heard him say that earlier. Now I know I *definitely* heard it.

I press my cheek even further into the seat, and I stab my finger to the screen of the Kindle. 15:37. Not long until four o'clock...

And this time when I look down and Sofie is staring at me, I don't nod at her, and I don't blink my eyes to tell her everything is going to be okay...

LENNY

15:37pm

Olette flicks a scarlet fingernail to the switch next to the steering wheel, then presses that fingernail to the button that winds the driver's side window down with a smooth swoosh.

'That's a relief,' Lenny says as Olette stretches to snatch the blue bulb from the roof, tossing it over her shoulder and into the back seat.

'Your ears get numb to the noise,' Olette says. 'There's no need for us to have the siren on... not while we're... driving.... waiting...'

They were driving the labyrinth of yellow fields north of Prague, until they heard more from Liam and Sofie, confident they were within pouncing distance. Olette had realised as soon as Liam texted through that they were being driven amongst yellow fields that they had to be north of Prague, driving the narrow countryside roads that stretch all the way to where the German and Polish borders split, where the fields are a peculiar bright yellow for the six months of spring and summer.

To focus, Lenny was squinting through the parched yellow

fields at the crooked line of the horizon, desperately hoping to see the shape of a blue car form somewhere within it.

'Didn't have you down as a field agent, Olette,' he says.

'Didn't have you down as finding two swiped children in the first few hours of starting with the PTU, Lenny. Not when the top of your head was sweating this morning walking into that interview.' She shrugs. 'Any update?' she asks, nodding at Lenny's lap, chicaning the conversation.

He picks up his phone, thumbs the screen, then shakes his head.

'Nothing yet,' he says. 'Not since Liam texted us saying they are somewhere in amongst the yellow fields. At this stage shouldn't we just... shouldn't we just get police to flood these roads?'

'Lenny,' Olette says, as the BMW whizzes over another dip in the tarmac. 'We're on top of this Horata guy. He doesn't even know we're on top of him. We know his name. We know what he looks like. We have text access to the two children he swiped this morning. We'll get him. We'll get them. We'll save them, Lenny.'

'But we'll... we'll save them quicker if we have more men on the ground.'

'Men, Lenny... Really?'

Lenny holds his eyes closed.

'Men *and* women, I mean. Olette, let's just make a call and—

'Lenny, when we rescue these two children from the jaws of being trafficked, the PTU can use the case to prove to donors that we work.'

'I knew it,' Lenny says, shaking his head. 'Didn't take an investigator to work that out, did it? This is about money. Not about Liam and Sofie.'

'Everything we do is for Liam and Sofie. And all of the Liams and Sofies, every day. Trust me. That's what we do. Every day, Lenny. Listen, if the local police find these two children, it'll be the bureaucratic system winning. If we find them, it'll mean millions. Multiple millions in donations for the PTU... Lenny...' she says, pressing a long fingernail to his thigh, staring her oversized marble eyeballs at his nubbed profile. 'This will be a major breakthrough for the PTU. Let's go find these two children. When we do, you will get all the credit you deserve for the great investigating you have done. Not the bureaucratic system. But you... A private investigator with the PTU. You'll deserve it.' She pinches his phone from his lap, then drops it back down, causing Lenny to bend forward.

'Ouch,' he says.

When his seatbelt snaps him back to the seat, he squints the length of the long tarmac road ahead of him as it wiggles through the yellow fields before checking the time on the digital dashboard behind Olette's steering wheel. 15:39. He's quite literally been on the road since he finished his interview at 9:45 am this morning. Five hours travelling. By jittering metro. By uncomfortable shoe. And now, by air-conditioned BMW. Zipping through the yellow fields that lead to Central Europe.

He notices, next to the clock, a button. A big red button marked 'GO'. Like something he'd expect on a kids toy.

'That's all you gotta do to start this car?' he asks. 'Press GO?'

'Sure is,' Olette replies, staring back at him. She seemed to be staring at Lenny as much as she was staring at the road ahead. 'You look very warm in that yellow jacket. Have done since I met you this morning.'

Lenny curls the corner of his lip and puffs a laugh through his nostrils before glancing at her pretty profile when she turns away.

'It's for luck,' he says.

Then they both stare toward the horizon, hoping to see a car form within it. A blue car.

'What if we're going in the wrong direction?' he asks.

'Lenny!' Olette huffs his name. 'You've been following your instinct all morning. Liam told us he saw yellow fields. As far as he could see. They have to be north... towards the Melnik. There are acres of yellow fields north of Kobylisy. Splinters of narrow roads like this one.'

'Where do the roads lead to?' Lenny asks, thumbing his screen to search Google Maps.

'Well,' Olette says. 'If we continue going north we'll end up in a three-country border split with Poland and Germany.'

'Jesus,' Lenny says.

'From there... who knows,' Olette continues. 'From Poland, the Eastern European market opens up. From Germany, western-Europe opens.'

'And there are markets for kidnapped children both ways?'

'Nobody ever believes how prevalent people trafficking is throughout Europe,' Olette says, turning her marble eyes his way again. 'Three hundred thousand children are reported missing every year through the continent, Lenny. That's nearly six thousand every month. Or, eight hundred and twenty-five every day. Or... ready for this....' She glances at the narrow road in front, then turns to Lenny again. 'Thirty-four children every hour. That means fifteen kids have gone missing in the half an hour we've been in this car together...'

Lenny blows out his cheeks.

'I read those stats on your website. And Dr Volgt reminded me of them in the interview this morning... But all of those children aren't taken for trafficking purposes, right?'

'Course not,' Olette hisses. 'Half of missing children turn up the next day, in a friend of a friend's house. Of the other half reported missing, the statistics vary country-to-country, society-to-society, between children who choose to run away—to get away from a life they don't want, and those who are swiped for trafficking purposes. The bottom line as far as the PTU is concerned? We believe three hundred children are swiped through the continent every day for the purpose of being sold on... sold into dark markets. The board's job is to try to find those three hundred cases every day out of the thousands of missing children cases reported. Not as easy as it sounds, is it? After the board go through all of the cases, they get a PI like you to chase down the clue that led them to declaring it a possible trafficking case.' Lenny nods his head slowly, rounding his chin. 'That figure, Lenny... of three hundred legitimate swiped children every day,' Olette continues. 'Is only getting bigger. That's why we've got to hire as many PIs as we can. That's why you're here right now. The board of the PTU spend the early morning going through the thousands of missing children cases, trying to locate the three-hundred that might be trafficking. Then later that morning, they send as many individual private investigators out to as many of the cases as they possibly can... Sometimes newly-hired investigators, just like you. Too much of everybody's time at the PTU is taken up with new recruits...'

Lenny squints into the horizon until his eyes start blinking. Then the lines on his forehead begin to splinter.

'Can't the PTU operate better than that?'

'Oh, we do,' Olette says. 'But you're at the, uh.... The bottom rung, right? No offence. The very top investigators at the PTU are in deep investigative territory, right at the very heart of people trafficking. Some are working undercover. At your level, Lenny, you get the off-chance possible child trafficking case before local police get involved. Let's just say it's the rat race of investigative practice at the PTU... Some investigators get deep into it, end up promoting themselves into the Unit... Some don't even last a month. I know you've been warned. Everybody at the PTU is warned. This is no easy sport.'

'Sure fucking isn't,' Lenny whispers.

Olette braces herself as the car zips over another dip in the tarmac.

'But you've made it look easy, Lenny,' she says. 'I'm impressed. The PTU's lead to you was Ruthgar Bilic. Guy comes up clean.

Investigation is normally over at that point. But you... you went and contacted the missing child, how about that?'

Lenny stifles a smirk, then twists his neck side-to-side to frighten the pride away.

'I bet you've got kids, right?' she asks.

Lenny blinks twice, then nods.

'Twin boys. Jared and Jacob.'

'How old?'

'Almost ten'

'Ouch,' she says. 'I bet they're a handful.'

Lenny curls the side of his mouth into a smile as the car leaps another dip in the tarmac road.

'You? Children?'

'No,' Olette says, shaking her head, then pushing out a laugh. 'Hell no.'

Lenny's lip retains its smile at her curt reply before he suddenly gets distracted by the screen lighting in his lap.

'Holy shit,' he says swiping his phone up. 'It's them. It's Liam.'

He holds a breath while he reads.

He is speaking in Czech on the phone. I can't understand him. But I did hear him say Flat Four in Labe. At 4 o'clock. He said that lots of times. Flat Four and Labe. 4 o'clock.

Olette punches her foot to the brake, causing Lenny to snap forward and then backwards into his seat, then they both stare at the digits on her dashboard.

15:40.

'Flat Four and Labe?' Olette says, lifting her glare to meet Lenny's beady, sunken eyes. 'Flat Four and Labe? Labe. Labe is the river.'

'The river?' Lenny says, his voice high-pitched. 'They're going by boat?'

Olette unbuckles her belt, turns in the front seat and crawls onto all fours, her backside wiggling next to Lenny's face.

When she transition-drops, almost effortlessly, back into the front seat in one twist-and-land, she blows away a strand of hair caught in her mouth then winds her window down, stretching to stab the blue bulb to the roof.

'They're going to the River Labe,' she says, winking at him.

She leans forward, flicks her long fingernail at the switch, and stamps on the gas as the siren pierces around them.

'How long's the River Labe?' Lenny shouts as he is sucked into his seat.

LIAM

The quiet since the engine turned off is scary. So scary I start to wish I could hear the tick-tock of the indicators again. And the car still moving. Zooming through the roads that brought us here. Wherever here is. Maybe it's Flat Four and Labe. If it is, Lenny Moon will be here soon. To save us. I'm sure that's what I heard him say. He said it lots of times. 'Flat Four and Labe. Ctyri hodin.'

I roll over a little, as quietly as I can, to look at him with one eye. He's sitting still in the front seat, one hand stroking his beard. The other on the steering wheel even though we're not driving anymore. He's waiting... waiting on something. Waiting on someone... I press at the Kindle again. Just to check the time. 15:45.

I swallow, and then I roll back away from him, and bow down to look at Sofie again. I can only see her if I bow down really low, squashing my chin into my neck. She has her eyes closed now. Is probably thinking what I'm thinking... that it would be less scary if we were still driving.

I'd like to rise up. Do a press up. To stare out the window. To see if I can see the flats. To see if there is one more clue that I can text to Lenny Moon. But I just keep my cheek pressed into the smelly back seat, and I, like, wait... and wait... To see where he has taken us. Or waiting for the Kindle to blink. Or for Lenny to drive around the corner. Whichever comes first...

I hear Sofie swallowing, and then it goes quiet. Really quiet. And I close my eyes. With my eyes closed I begin to hear a slap. A silent slap. Like a slap, slap, slap noise. Over and over again. I know that sound. I've heard it before. Lots of times. In the background. A silent slap... slap... slap. Reminds me of home. Not my house. But down by the harbour. Slap... slap.

'Hmmm,' I say, inside my mouth. It makes Sofie look up at my face. But I look away from her and I can feel that my eyes are wide. Really wide. That's water! That's the sound of water. Lapping. Lap... lap... lap. *Definitely*! I look down at Sofie again and I nod. I nod to let her know that we have another clue. Then I roll over and I glance with one eye at him again, to see he still has one hand stretched to the steering wheel, the other stroking his beard. It's too quiet to text Lenny Moon back. When the car was moving, the engine was on, and the indicator was tick-tocking it was easier to text. I don't want to get caught. Not in the silence. But I have to, like, try. I have to try to text Lenny Moon and let him know we're near water. Like a lake. Or a river. Or a harbour. Or a sea. That will be a big clue. We must be near a flat by the water. Flat Four and Labe near some water. Lenny Moon will know... he'll have to know where we are.

I hold my eyes closed as I roll over the Kindle, then I stab a finger at the screen, making it glow again, my belly hiding it from the man with the dirty beard. I keep my arm tight to my side, my finger stretching to type when suddenly he moves in the front seat. His jacket swishing. And moving. Turning. Then... snatching the front door open. My body rolls over the Kindle and stiffens. And I hold my eyes closed before I hear the door slam shut. Then there are voices. Outside. He's talking... Talking to somebody. In Czech.

I press my hand to the smelly seat and lift myself, opening my eyes to stare out the side window. We're not near any flats. But we are near water. Like a big lake. Or a river. But there are no flats. There are no buildings at all around here. Nothing. Yellow fields and a river. And I start to think I gave Lenny Moon a wrong clue. I told him we were going to Flat Four. But we're not. We're just at some lake, or river.

I land back down on the seat and stab at the Kindle again, then begin typing as quickly as I can. I text Lenny that I hear water. And see water. But no flats. Just countryside. Yellow fields and a big lake. I'm tapping my finger against the Kindle, trying to finish the text when the back door snatches open, and it gets really cold really quickly. Like an icy wind. Really windy. And cold.

'How old are you, girl?' the man with the dirty beard asks as I lean over the Kindle.

I bow down to look at Sofie, and I see her neck swallowing before she tries to speak. But nothing comes out of her mouth. Just a 'hmmm' inside her own head. I know that sound. It's the only sound I can make, too when I try to talk. The man with the dirty beard reaches toward her face, then rips the Sellotape back really quickly.

'Ayyy!' Sofie says, before she starts kissing at her own lips.

'How old are you, girl?'

'Seven,' Sofie says. 'Seven.'

'And you!'

He steps into the back of the car, kneeling over me before ripping the tape from my lips. The pain makes me suck in through my teeth, then I breathe in and out of my mouth really quick. As if I've never breathed in and out of my mouth before...

'Nine,' I eventually say.

He steps out without saying anything else.

'Sedem a devet,' I hear him tell the other man.

'Devet?' the strange voice says. 'Devet?'

The door slams shut again. And I bow to stare down at Sofie, to see her licking her own lips.

'Hey,' I whisper.

'Hello,' she says, staring up at me.

'Don't worry, Lenny Moon is on his way. He's right behind us. He was in the house we were taken from. I told him we were driving in yellow fields. And I'm about to tell him we're near water. Near a lake or a river. He's coming, Sofie.'

'That's so good,' she says. Her voice is squeaky. Just like Yvonne's.

'My little sister is six. She looks a bit like you. She sounds like you. I'm going to look after you, Sofie. Like a brother. Until Lenny Moon gets here.'

She nods. And smiles.

'Thank you,' she says. 'What's your name—

The back door snatches open again, and as I bow down further, squashing my throat, I see him, the man with the dirty beard, pulling Sofie out of the car.

SOFIE

I scream. Then when I look down, I am standing. Standing on the yellow grass. A hand goes over my mouth. And I stare at Liam still lying on the backseat before the car door slams shut. And he's left inside on his own. And I'm out here with two men standing over me. One of them holding his dirty hand across my mouth.

'If you stay quiet, I will not hurt you,' the man with the beard says from behind me. He takes his hand away, and I twist around to look at him. To see if I can see his eyes. But he doesn't look back at me. He doesn't want to look back at me. Then I look up at the other man. The other man doesn't have a full beard. Just a little one. A short, wispy grey one. And long brown hair that is grey around his ears. I look at both of their faces. Then at the two boats behind them. Bobbling up and down on a river. A big river. And I already know I'm going in one of the boats. And I start to shake. Not just because I am scared. But because of the cold. It's so, so cold down by the river. And the wind doesn't stop.

'Tu es stupide, Sofie!' I whisper. Quietly. So, so quietly that the men can't hear me over the noise of the wind.

I look back over my shoulder at the blue car. Hoping Liam is looking at me through the window. Nodding at me. Telling me everything is going to be okay. That private investigator Lenny Moon is coming to save us. To save us before we are taken away on to these two boats.

But there's nobody in the window. Liam is lying down. Scared. Scared and shaking as much as I am.

I wipe my eyes into my shoulders so that I don't cry, and then I look around. At the yellow fields past the blue car that lead all the way to the river. At the opposite side of the river, a long, long way away. I see a signpost. A brown signpost. It's small. But I can read it.

Vlatva & Labe

'Ona mluví česky?' the man with long hair asks.

The man with the beard looks at me.

'What languages you speak?'

'English et francais,' I say.

The two men shrug at each other and then they stare out at the river again. As if they're waiting on the boats to do something.

The man with the long brown hair asks another question, but I don't hear it. Not over the wind. Even if I did hear it, I wouldn't be able to understand it. Then, suddenly, the man with the beard walks past me and reaches for the door of the blue car, pulling it open.

I feel better when Liam is pulled onto his feet, but he's not as quiet as I was. He's screaming. And shouting. And then the man with the beard grabs him from behind, twisting him.

'Ah, okay... right. I'm sorry,' Liam says, before he drops to his knees. 'Ouch!'

'I will get more tape and put it across your mouth. Be quiet, you understand?'

Liam nods his head. And I look around, to see if there are any people in the yellow fields who heard Liam screaming and shouting. But it's empty around here. Just yellow fields. In a strong wind. I think about shouting and screaming too, to see if anybody will hear me. But I don't want the man with the beard to squeeze my neck like he squeezed Liam's.

And I shiver again. With the scare. And the cold.

'Jak je starý?' the long-haired man says.

'Devet,' the bearded man says.

'Devet? Devet je prilis stare!'

I don't know what they are talking about, but they both look angry. And then the man with the beard leans closer to the man with the long hair and they talk louder in each other's faces. I take a small step backwards, then another one. I look over my shoulder at Liam as he is getting to his feet, rubbing the back of his neck.

'Are you okay?' I whisper to him.

'Yeah,' he says back to me, sucking in through his teeth.

He steps forward and stands beside me while the two men keep shouting.

'Sofie,' Liam whispers, 'we got to get that Kindle from the car. That's what will save us. Especially if they're going to take us away in those...' He nods towards the boats behind the two men, and suddenly the shiver goes through my whole body. All the way down to my toes. Liam puts an arm around my shoulder and squeezes me tight before letting go. It was only a quick hug. So, so quick. But it made me feel safer. It made me feel warmer. And I stop shivering. Nobody ever hugs me. Nobody...

'I'll stand here,' he whispers, 'and while they're shouting at each other, you go back to the car and get the Kindle.'

'Me?' I say.

'If they put us on different boats, you'll need it, Sofie.'

I close my eyes, and when I open them I spin around to look at the blue car. The back door is still open. From when the man with the beard pulled Liam out. I can't see it from here, but I know that the Kindle is on the backseat. Liam had been lying on it when I was pulled from the car.

'Okay,' I whisper back, before turning to see the men still shouting at each other. The man with the beard is pointing his finger now, shaking his head.

I take a big step backwards, then another before reaching the open door of the car and holding my fingers to it. Then I take one more big backwards step and suddenly I can sit on the back seat, my legs out of the car.

The men are talking now. Not shouting. Just talking. And the man with the beard puts his hand over his face. That's when I lean backwards, my shoulders touching the smelly back seat. I push myself back with my feet, until I can feel it... until I can grip the Kindle.

'Ayyyyy!' the man with the beard shouts.

I sit straight back up, the Kindle pinched between my fingers, to see him stomping towards me. 'What are you doing? I told you to stay still. Stay still or I will hurt you.'

He reaches for my shoulder, then pulls me out of the car, and I fall to my knees, the Kindle spilling from my fingers, tumbling to the yellow grass.

I hear the man with the beard bend down, and when I look over my shoulder, he is picking the Kindle up.

LENNY

15:50pm

'There aren't many flat complexes on the riverbanks,' Lenny shouts over the siren, his fingers pinching in and out of the map on his phone, 'though this river sure does travel. It goes for miles, Olette. Forty-miles. Then it splinters off into all sorts of streams.'

Olette grips the steering wheel tight as she continues to zip the car through the tarmac roads, navigating her way through the web of yellow fields towards the River Labe.

'Flat Four?' she says robotically—as if she is zoned to another channel, her mind whirring as fast as the tyres beneath her. 'Flat Four? Flat Four?'

'Let's just, at this stage, ring the police,' Lenny shouts. 'We can have every block of flats along the river searched as soon as possible and...look it's ten to four now!'

Olette shakes her head subtly before turning to face Lenny.

'We can find them, Lenny. You and me. We can—'

'Call the police, Olette!' he shouts over her. 'We need as many feet on the ground as we can get. Or boats in rivers. Or cars on roads... whatever we need.'

Olette nudges her foot to the brake, slowing the car down until it eventually stops, then she flicks her fingernail against the switch, killing the wail that had been piercing, before blinking her large marble eyes at her passenger.

'But... what information do we give the police, other than what we've already got?'

'It's not about the information,' Lenny says. 'It's about the feet on streets... we need more eyes. Now! We've narrowed the search down to somewhere along the River Labe. The more eyes we have on the river, *in* the river... the easier it will be to find these kids.'

'But we're so close, Lenny,' she says. 'It would mean so much to the PTU if you found them... If a PTU investigation came up with the goods in this case. New recruit. Finds two swiped children on his first day. Just think of the exposure this would get you. Get us...'

'Olette,' Lenny says, his eyes blinking with frustration, 'First and foremost, these kids have to be found... It doesn't matter who gets the credit. I don't care if it's me. The PTU. Or the Czech police force. Liam and Sofie need to be found. Now! Do it. Call 'em. Call the police.'

Olette exhales a groan, then pulls her phone from her pocket, irritation etched into the vertical crease above the bridge of her nose.

'Lenny... if they're getting away by speedboat along the Labe they could end up anywhere. They could be in Germany or Poland by sundown. They could even be heading south... They could be in Austria or Slovakia by tonight. This is a PTU case.'

'That's why we need eyes. Because they could end up anywhere soon,' Lenny says.

Olette reaches her hand to Lenny's shoulder and widens her glossy eyes at him.

'Lenny, if you only knew about the bureaucracy. The politics. The bullshit of it all.'

'Call the police, Olette.'

'Police don't have river boats, Lenny! They don't have speedboats. In Florida... in California... in the movies you watched when you were a kid, maybe. Here, in the centre of Europe, we have bureaucracy. Stinking bureaucracy. If we call the police, they'll do nothing. They can't do anything... They might, after fifteen phone calls, get a small motorboat in a certain area of the Labe, but Lenny listen to me... police boats can't go through borders. This is what I mean by bureaucracy. It's bureaucracy that fails these states, these lands. These countries. Three hundred children are kidnapped for trafficking purposes every single day through Europe. Why do you think the PTU had to be set up in the first place? It's because the bureaucratic system fails missing children... It's pretty much set up to fail them. It fails us all. Police can't get involved for the first crucial twenty-four hours. When they do, their policing stops at the borders, land, or sea. The systemic bureaucracy is everything the PTU stands against, Lenny. We demand a better system. We demand more respect for the people trafficking that happens across Europe every single day... Look,' she shouts, pointing a long fingernail at the digits on the dashboard. 15:51. 'We've been in the car for fifty-minutes now. Over a dozen children have been kidnapped for people trafficking purposes since we've been sat on these leather seats... Wanna know how many men or women in police uniforms are tracking them down? Zero! None! Why not? Bureaucracy, Lenny. And every time we let bureaucracy win, we are getting further and further away from what the PTU were set up to do in the first place. Which is to stop child trafficking. Not help it by turning a blind eye for the first twenty-four hours.'

Lenny shakes his bald head, before stretching to tap his index finger against the phone Olette is gripping.

'That's why we have to phone the police,' he says, stabbing

the same digits Olette had just pointed at. 15:51. 'If something is happening at four o'clock we don't have long. Call the police, Olette. Tell them to check all flat complexes along the river. You know it's the right thing to do.'

Olette puffs her cheeks, turns her phone over in her hand, then taps a finger gingerly against it before bringing a ringing tone to her ear, eyeballing Lenny as she does so.

'Dobry den, police Zdarski,' Lenny hears a voice say when the ring tone cuts.

'Ahoj,' Olette says, 'Mama pohotovost...'

As Olette begins to explain the situation in Czech, Lenny picks his phone up from his lap and begins to zoom in on his map, scrolling tentatively along the River Labe and squinting at the array of streams that spray from it.

He listens back into Olette's phone call, hearing her mention 'Flat Four and Labe,' and when he returns to the streams on his screen before that screen begins to sizzle in his hand.

He punches his thumb against the green circle, then brings the screen to his ear.

'Hello,' he says.

'Hul-lo,' she says. 'How are you Len-ny?'

'Great. Mad, actually. Crazy what's going on... I, uh... I wouldn't even know where to begin, Celina.'

'The boys are having lunch. Mash and beans. I just wanted to ring to see... to say... to ask how you are doing?'

Lenny blows out his cheeks and scratches the stubble above his ear.

'Grand, Celina. I mean... actually...' he washes a hand over his face, 'I don't know how I'm doing to be honest. I dunno.'

'That's okay,' Celina says. 'You just think about doing your job. I shouldn't have... I shouldn't have called you in the middle of an investigation. I should... I should go.'

Lenny stares at Olette, still rapping Czech as fast as she can into her phone.

'Celina, look,' he says, slowly, 'you can call me anytime. You'll give the boys a kiss and a hug from me tonight again, yeah?'

'Of course I will, Len-ny. We, eh... we miss you, but we don't want you to come home. Not until you've done your job. We're proud of you, Len-ny.'

'That means a lot, Celina. I, uh... I... I'm proud of you, too.'

He sucks and holds a quiet breath in the resulting silence, not even noticing that Olette has hung up her call and is now glaring her huge eyes at him.

'Well, guess we'll see you tomorrow,' Celina says.

'Yeah... I'll see you tomorrow. I, uh... I, I... L-look, er.... thank you.'

A dead tone throbs in Lenny's ear, and when it stops, he realises he's sitting in silence before he hears the flicker of eyelashes.

'Your wife?' she asks.

'No,' he says.

'Girlfriend?' Lenny shakes his head. 'You sure?'

'Hmm, hmm,' he replies, nodding. 'What did the police say?'

'I called the chief of the northern territory. He's not sure what the protocol is for river searches exactly, but he's making a call to a man who knows the man who knows all about it. Bureaucracy, Lenny. I told you. This is the pace the bureaucratic system works at. Red tape after red tape. I mentioned Flat Four and Labe. He was as bewildered as we are. But he can get a dozen patrol men and women searching flat complexes along the banks of the Labe within the next half hour.'

'Deadly,' Lenny says, his bald head still nodding.

'Shame for you to do all of the leg work on this investigation only for some officer in a uniform to front the press conference on tonight's news...'

Lenny shrugs.

'Well,' he says, 'I guess we have as much chance of finding Sofie and Liam as any of those patrol guys... At least we have more people on the streets now. Searching. Looking. How far are we from the River Labe now?'

Olette huffs, her bottom lip sticking out.

'Ten minutes,' she says, guessing.

'Let's get to it then,' Lenny says.

Olette stabs her finger at the GO button, making the engine purr, then she flicks the switch to wail the siren again.

'What are the names of the entry points to the lake?' Lenny shouts as the car takes off.

'By boat?' Olette shouts back.

'Yeah. If they're going to be taken by boat, where would be the best point in the lake to take them on board?'

'There are lots of entry points along the River Labe,' Olette shouts. 'But the main places are ports such as Brunsbuttel. Butzfleth. Dresden. Dresden's a good size port actually. There's Ostermort, too, of course. Witnneberg is another big port. That's one of the biggest actually.'

'Not a big port,' Lenny shouts. 'That would make what they're doing noticeable. They'll wanna get kids on their boats without being noticed. I'm wondering about entry points that are discreet. Secret entry points for boats. If you were trying to traffic people, where would the best place be along the River Labe to get away? Somewhere where the river splits, right?'

Olette blows out her lips, her chin rounded as she nods.

'I don't know, Lenny. Not really. That river is a thoroughfare to Europe. There are a number of points it splinters off into different directions. There's a bend at Rousell which would be discreet and takes off in two different directions. It's similar at Hornafen, too. The river splits there like a prong. It splits at Vltava too. And at Spitze.'

Lenny's face darts towards Olette.

'Wait... what? Go back... What did you just say?'

'Spitze.'

'No,' Lenny shakes his head. 'The one before that.'

'Vlatva. Where Vltava meets Labe. The rivers split into all sorts of streams from a u-bend at Vlatva.'

'Vltava?'

'Yeah,' Olette says, her head nodding, her brow creasing.

'Vlat-va,' Lenny repeats. Slower this time.

'Shit!' Olette shouts, the penny dropping, her foot pressing the gas pedal to its flattest point, pinning Olette and Lenny back into their seats. 'Vltava and Labe. Not Flat Four and Labe. Vlat-va. Vlatva and Labe. A u-bend where the Vlatva meets the Labe. We've got them, Lenny,' she says. 'I know exactly where that u-bend is!'

LIAM

The man with the dirty beard picks Sofie up gently, not like he picked me up by the back of the neck, and then he walks her towards me, his eyes staring down at the screen of the Kindle in his other hand.

I rub the back of my neck because it is still sore and I hope, I just hope that he can't see the messages Lenny Moon has been sending to me and Sofie. And then I realise that I shouldn't be rubbing my neck. My two hands are supposed to be tied. So, I drop my hand to my back and squish my two wrists together.

'Fucking books,' he says.

Then he drops the Kindle to the grass and walks over it, towards the man with the long hair he had been shouting at before he noticed Sofie was trying to take the Kindle out of the car.

I look at Sofie, then down at the Kindle beside her feet and I nod my head towards it, telling her to bend down, and pick it up. We need it. We need that Kindle. That is how Lenny Moon will find us.

She looks back at me. Scared. And I just nod down at the Kindle again, because we *have* to stay in contact with Lenny

Moon. We have to give him more clues to where we are. Where we are going. Unless he gets here first... To wherever here is. On the edge of this river, somewhere in the middle of these yellow fields.

Sofie takes a big breath in, then steps over the Kindle and crouches down, trying to feel for it on the grass with her hands tied behind her back. But she can't really reach... So, I walk towards her and take my eyes away from the men to stare down.

'Back a bit more,' I whisper.

Sofie falls backwards, and when she lands on her bum on the yellow grass, I look up at the two men staring out towards the river and when I see that they are not looking at us, I bend down and pick the Kindle up and shove it into Sofie's hands.

'Take it. Take it,' I say.

When she grips it, I put my hand under her armpit, and I lift her back to her feet before putting my hand behind my back and squishing my two wrists together.

'You okay?' I whisper.

'No. Are you?' she says.

I take my time before I answer her. Because I don't want to tell her the truth. I don't want to say 'no' like she did.

'We'll be fine,' I say, 'Lenny Moon will get here soon. He will. And he'll save us.'

The man with the dirty beard turns around and walks towards us, and as he does I stare into his eyes. But he doesn't look back into mine. He doesn't look at me or at Sofie. He walks past both of us. Then he slams the back door of the car closed and opens the front door before bending himself inside.

When he stands back up and turns around he is putting a cigarette to his mouth, trying to light it. But he can't seem to light it... not in the wind.

'Where is private investigator Lenny Moon now?' Sofie whispers.

I shrug my shoulders. Because I don't want to whisper back.

Not now that the man with the dirty beard is walking back past us, his cigarette pinched between his fingers, blowing a thick smoke cloud out of his mouth. When he is back talking with the other man, I turn to Sofie.

'Lenny Moon knows we were driving in these yellow fields. He can't be far away. He can't be... He'll have to drive down this road at some point....'

I look over my shoulder, trying to keep my wrists pressed together behind my back, and then Sofie looks over her shoulder and we both stare at the road we just drove down. It's empty and quiet. So empty and quiet it looks like nobody's ever going to drive down it. Even if we waited here for another ten days.

'He'll be here,' I whisper. Even though I don't believe myself. These yellow fields, they're everywhere. They go on as far as I can see. And even more than that. Because we spent a long, long time driving through them. Lenny Moon could be anywhere. He's not going to come driving down this road anytime soon. I know he's not. We need more clues. We need to give Lenny Moon more clues before we are taken on to those boats.

'Can you text him?' I whisper. 'Tell him we're near a river?'

'Vlatva and Labe,' Sofie whispers back.

'Huh?'

'Vlatva and Labe.... Look...'

She nods her head towards a brown signpost down by the river and I can tell her eyesight must be better than mine. Because I can barely see it. I definitely can't read it. But I try my best, and it is only because Sofie said it that I can make out the words. Or the shapes of the words. Vlatva. Vlatva and Labe. Not Flat Four and Labe. Vlatva. That's where we are. Vlatva.

'Great,' I say. A little bit too loud. I stand still, hoping the men didn't hear me. But they didn't. Not over the sound of the strong wind. 'Let's text that to Lenny Moon. Tell him we're at Vlatva and Labe. Right on the riverbank.'

'How am I supposed to text him?' she whispers really quietly.

Sofie seems scared. As if the men will catch us talking and then hurt us. So, I take a deep breath and stare down at the Kindle gripped in her tiny hands. And now I know I'll have to do it. I'll have to do it with my free hand. Without getting caught.

I look up at the two men staring out at the two boats bobbing on the river and then I take a step behind Sofie, tilting her hands down a little bit so I can see the screen. When I touch it, the screen lights up, and that's when I can touch the Customer Service chat button to get to the keyboard.

As soon as I start to type the two men turn around to us and I feel really scared. As if I've been caught.

'Okay, okay,' the man with the dirty beard says. 'You!' He points at me. 'That boat. You!' He points at Sofie. 'That boat. Go. Go on. Move!'

'Nooo!' Sofie shouts. 'No! Don't separate us— '

The man walks quickly towards us and slaps his hand over Sofie's mouth, and I take my loose hand away from my back and I try to grab him, grab him around the neck. Only the other man, the one with the long hair, grabs my arm. And grabs my shoulder.

'Ne. Ne. Ne,' he shouts in my ear.

He twists my hand around my back and begins to tie them back up with the rope still clung to my other hand. Tight. Really tight. As if he is trying to saw my wrists off with the rope.

'Owww,' I say.

'You shut up, too,' the man with the dirty beard says into my face. 'Otherwise we will hurt you. Both of you.'

When the man with the long hair has finished tying my hands tight, he pushes me forward, towards the first boat.

'Can't you keep us together? Please? Send us in the same boat? Please...'

'You were told to shut up,' the man with the beard says from behind, pushing Sofie forward, down the yellow grass mound that leads to the riverbank.

I look behind me, at Sofie. To make sure she still has the Kindle in her hands. She does, gripping it tight. Really tight.

Then suddenly she stops walking. Scared. Frightened. And then I get frightened because she is frightened. That's when I see what made her scared. Another man is walking towards us with a woolly hat on his head, carrying a black bag. As if he just walked out of the river.

He throws the bag to the grass in front of Sofie, and I try to look down into it, but it's closed.

The man with the dirty beard pushes Sofie forward, towards the man with the woolly hat. Then he bends down and picks the bag up and unzips it...

I stare up into his eyes while he looks in the bag. Then he glances up at me before his head darts over his shoulder. And suddenly Sofie's head turns, too. And I'm not sure what they've seen, or what they've heard until I close my eyes...and that's when it hits me. I can hear it, too. A siren. A siren coming for us. Coming to save us...

LENNY

16:03pm

The black BMW leaps over another dip in the road, all four of its tyres briefly lifting before slapping back to the tarmac, causing Lenny and Olette to jaunt forwards, then backwards in their seats.

Lenny's been gripping the handle above the passenger door, his jaw swinging from side-to-side as the siren pierces around him, a wave of tension washing through his stomach.

'One more minute!' Olette shouts.

Lenny doesn't react, staying focused on the horizon ahead, squinting along the crooked line where the yellow grass kisses the grey sky, waiting to see ripples of water.

The car slows its pace, Olette's foot easing from the pedal, before she drags the steering wheel left, following the road to the river. Then she presses down firmer again with her foot, the tyres screeching underneath as the engine growls, the car powering again, propelling them forward.

'There!' Lenny shouts out. His hand letting go of the handle to point through the windscreen. 'The river!'

He leans forward, his eyes squinting.

'Boats?' he whispers. 'Two boats!' he shouts.

Olette grits her teeth as she stamps downwards, her posture forward, willing the car to quicken.

'It's them!' she calls out, mirroring Lenny by pointing her hand forward. 'See?'

Lenny refocuses his squint, until he can make out the silhouettes of figures straight ahead. Two adult figures. Dragging two children?

The car leaps another dip in the road, and when it lands, Olette cuts the final bend in the tarmac by driving through the yellow grass, where the car crunches and then clunks before she snatches at the handbrake, skidding the black BMW to a stop just shy of the blue car they had been chasing.

Without hesitating, Lenny stabs his seatbelt button, then snatches the passenger door open before racing as fast as he can across the grass, the arms of his yellow puffer jacket whizzing either side of him. When he looks back, Olette is behind, panting, squeaking, sprinting as fast as she can. But it's not easy. Not in this muddy yellow grass.

'Go!' she shouts after Lenny.

He lengthens his stride and when he approaches the boat with the blue rim he hears a splash, causing him to dart his head left to where a woolly hat is bobbing up and down in the water, a bald man swimming away, swimming toward the opposite side of the river.

'You go to that boat!' Lenny shouts back towards Olette.

Then he whizzes his arms faster, sprinting towards the second boat when suddenly he hears a growl. Like a lawnmower. Roaring. Then grunting.

The boat he is racing towards rocks backwards, stuttering,

before it shoots forwards, its loud engine skimming it across the top of the choppy river.

Lenny widens his stride, puffing, huffing, and when he reaches the riverbank, he leaps, arms first, over the curved edge of land where the River Vltava meets the River Labe, before his yellow puffer jacket slaps against the cold, grey water.

When his bald head reaches above the lapping current, he spits a mouthful of River back into the river before spinning in a circle, round, and round, until he can see the speedboat he was diving towards racing away from him, spraying cold, grey water back into his face.

He slaps the river with both arms, then grunts before turning toward the boat that didn't move; didn't move because its skipper jumped overboard as Lenny was approaching. He squints through the river, searching for the bald man, seeing him as a dot in the distance. Many strokes away. Way too many strokes for Lenny to make up.

He wipes his eyes with his fingers as he bobs on the river, then sees Olette jumping over the large blue rim of the first speedboat, gripping the bars.

When he looks back over the bloated shoulder of his puffer jacket, he sees the other boat is almost out of sight. Who did he think he was? Trying to out-swim a speedboat?

He slaps the river with both puffed arms again, then dives forward, swooping under the water, then arriving back up and bob-swimming toward the riverbank he had foolishly leaped from.

He grabs a handful of yellow grass, before heaving himself up, arriving on all fours in a mudded mess on the edge of the riverbank, panting and puffing and spitting into the puddle beneath him.

'I got one,' Olette shouts over the blast of the wind. 'We got one of the kids!'

Lenny lifts his right hand up and punches the air in half-celebration.

And when he rests it back down so he's steady on all fours again, still puffing and panting, his gut churns, and he heaves, spitting and burping. He pivots his head slowly, staring down river where the speedboat he thought he could out-swim is now totally out of sight.

'I need to know where that boat's going,' he whispers to himself. 'We gotta... I gotta... we gotta—' He heaves into the muddy puddle beneath him. Exhausted. Exasperated. His jacket weighing like a mattress around him, his tight navy suit trousers clinging to his skinny legs.

He sucks heavy breaths as deep as he can into his lungs, then huffs them out. In... and then out..... Until his throat fills, choking him, squeezing his neck tight....

He tries to cough, then panics, before it rushes through him —a chestful of river, projectiling to the puddle below.

He finally exhales a satisfied breath. As if a weight has lifted. A weight of river.

And when his breathing finally settles and steadies, he looks over his opposite shoulder at the boat Olette is on, wondering which child she is hugging right now... wondering which one of the two children got lucky.

He kicks one foot into the centre of his four-legged pose, then pushes his two hands firmer to the muddied grass, heaving himself back to his feet, water pouring from him as he stands upright. Then he pats down his jacket, squeezing as much of the river from him as he can.

'Fuck!' he whispers, slapping his palm against his pocket, before diving his hand inside and gripping his phone.

When he palms it, he stares at the screen. It's still on. Still alight. He thumbs it. Then thumbs it again. And again. And again...

'Shit, shit, shit,' he repeats. 'Bollocks! The phone is jammed.'

He wraps his two hands around the phone, then snaps it open, separating the battery from the screen, before bringing his hands to his mouth, huffing, and puffing as much hot air into them as he can muster.

When he shovels the screen into one pocket of his yellow jacket and the battery into the other, as if keeping them separate will somehow suck out the river, he looks back up the stretch of river again, as if by some miracle the speedboat with the missing child is going to miraculously turn back around. He then swivels back and begins walking towards the boat with the blue rim; the boat Olette is on, hugging the lucky child.

He stops... squints through the river in search of the bald man who braved a long swim. But he can't see anything. The river is too grey. Too choppy. Too vast. The bald man would have to be a good swimmer to make it to the other side. Certainly a better swimmer than Lenny has ever been. Though that wouldn't be tough.

'I gotta know where that second speedboat is travelling to,' Lenny whispers to himself as he sludges his way towards the boat with the blue rim.

'Hey!' he calls out over the strong wind as he stumbles forward. 'Which kid did we save?'

He stretches to his tip-toes on the muddy riverbank, to peer over the rim of the speedboat, seeing the top of Olette's head.

Then, his stare darts over his shoulder. A noise. A growl. The growl of an engine. He stands, stunned, as the blue car reverses, then screeches around the black BMW. Lenny glares through the side window as it speeds through the yellow grass, making its way to the tarmac road, seeing a grey-brown matted beard framing the profile of a face he's seen before. The face on a strip of three passport photographs that are currently lying soaked inside the pocket of his yellow puffer jacket. The face of Javi Horata. The man who swiped Sofie and Liam from the northern streets of

Prague this morning. The man who knows where that second boat is travelling to.

'Heyyy!' Lenny shouts. 'Horata. Stop! You are under arrest!'

He tries to run, but the mud grips him, tripping him back onto all fours. He sucks his right leg from the sludge, before pulling it forward. Then he crawls through the thickness of the muddied mess until he can get his feet on the more solid ground of soaked yellow grass. As he rises, he sees the blue car whizzing up the tarmac road he and Olette had raced down just minutes ago, racing away from him. Getting further and further away... He paces as fast as his heavy legs can take him across the yellow grass, towards the black BMW.

'These fucking shoes,' he shouts to himself as he limps to a stop, stretching for the door. When he yanks it open, he turns around to face the speedboat with the blue rim, to see Olette is standing now, hugging the child they rescued. Lenny squints, to see who it is, but he can't quite make the figure out, not pressed so tightly to Olette's bosom. So he pivots and drops, squelching his backside into the driver's seat of the BMW, and slapping the door closed.

He slides his seatbelt across his chest, slots it into the catch and then stretches his finger for the GO button before stabbing it, making the car purr. When he steps on the gas, the tyres spin on the yellow grass before jumping forward, causing the car to crunch and croak until it reaches the smoothness of the tarmac road.

'I have to fucking get this guy,' he says, clicking the gear stick downwards, then stepping on the gas firmer, the car zipping through the tarmac. In chase of a blue car; the blue car he now knows for certain is around the next bend, or perhaps the bend after that. Horata has about a ninety-second head start on Lenny. In a smaller, inferior car...

'I gotta catch this bastard,' Lenny shouts.

To be continued....

WHATEVER HAPPENED TO JAVI HORATA?

Book Five
in
The Lenny Moon Series.

Check out the opening chapter on the next page.

JAVI

I did not want to take them. That is the truth. The real truth. If I had the choice to be a normal man with a normal job and normal family and a normal life, then I would not have taken them. Honest to God above, I would not have taken them.

I am not a bad man. Or I used to not be a bad man. Before today. But I just... it was just so easy. Like taking candy from a baby. Or giving candy to a baby. Which is what I did.

I look over my shoulder. Into the back seat of the car and I stare at the satchel. Again. Then I stare above it, out the back window. To make sure that man in the ugly yellow jacket isn't following me. He jumped into the river. Thinking he could catch up with a speedboat. I saw him trying to get out two minutes later. Gripping onto the grass. That's when I thought I better run for it. I better get to the car. Get out of here as soon as I could.

Honest to God above, I am not a bad man. I am not. I just needed that satchel. It's the other people who are the bad people. The people who run corporations. The people who run big businesses. The people who run politics. They are the ones who make sure the little people like me can't get jobs. Can't afford houses. Can't afford dinners.

That's why I had those mints on me this morning. I found them when I was looking through the bins for some food. For some fruit. I usually find half-eaten apples in the bin. Sometimes some unfinished fast food still in the container. That's my favourite find. Because fast food stays warm when it is in a container.

I just need to think about that satchel. That way I will forget about those two children. I will forget their little faces. The dry tears on their cheeks.

She was happy and smiley at first. She was actually happy that I was talking to her. That I offered her a mint. Then when I suggested she come to my car for more candy, she came with me... She walked right behind me all the way to the car. That's how easy it was. I didn't mean to take a kid today. I was just walking towards the orphanage. To see how easy it might be. To see if I could do it. To see if I could really carry it out if it ever came to that. It was easy to buy the rope and the black duct tape. Anybody can do that. I had it in my car for two weeks before today. I bought it in Gnacko's Hardware. For just eight euros. Thinking one day I might try it. One day I might try to snatch a kid. Just so I could start a proper life.

I would not have known about snatching kids if I had never been in prison. In prison you learn all sorts of new tricks. How silly is it to gather all of the criminals together, and put them in the same building for twenty-four hours a day? How idiotic are the people who run prisons? Who run politics? How fucking idiotic can they be? I would never have thought of snatching a kid if it wasn't for the ugly men I met behind bars. It was sitting on the benches at the canteen in C-Wing of Pankrac prison where I learned about the market. That's where I first heard that you can make ten times more money from snatching a kid than you can by holding up a bank. Or a post office. And it's easier. Much easier. And less risky. There are cameras all over banks and post offices. That's how I got caught the last time. But in the fields, in the suburbs, there are no cameras. There are no risks. Not really.

It's as simple as stealing candy from a baby. Or giving candy to a baby. Which is what I did. And now I have fifty thousand euro filling the satchel in the backseat of the car I stole yesterday.

I am literally on my way to starting a new life. I'm going back to Portugal. Back to where it all began for me. Before I ran away. Before I ran away from my father's fists. And his belts. I can still feel his belts whipping my back anytime I think back that far. I can feel that pain anytime I want...

I stare into the rear-view mirror to see that the narrow road behind me is still empty. That idiot in the yellow jacket is nowhere near me. I'll be out of these country fields in twenty-minutes. Then out of Prague twenty-minutes after that. Then out of this country one more hour after that. Then I'll be free... free to start the life I should have started years ago, years before I started getting into trouble.

It is just a shame I had to steal two children to start this life. I didn't want to take them... I didn't. I was just walking. Honest to God above, I was just walking through the fields towards the orphanage. To see if it was easy to snatch a kid. To see if kids might fracture and split up. To see if it was possible to find one walking alone. When I did see one walking alone. About a mile before I reached the orphanage. Walking straight towards me. A little blonde. Tiny, tiny little girl.

'Would you like a mint?' I asked her.

She didn't pause.

She stuck out her hand. And I pulled the mints out of my pocket and popped one from the top for her to take.

Her face went all funny as she sucked on it.

'It's nice,' she then said.

I looked around the fields. It was just the two of us. Just me and the tiny, little blonde. And all I saw was fifty-thousand euro.

'You hungry?' I asked.

'I'm really hungry,' she said.

'Okay,' I said, my heart thumping. 'Follow me.'

FROM INTERNATIONAL BESTSELLING AUTHOR

DAVID B. LYONS

WHATEVER HAPPENED TO JAVI HORATA?

BOOK FIVE OF THE LENNY MOON NOVELLA SERIES

WHATEVER HAPPENED TO JAVI HORATA?

The End.

ACKNOWLEDGMENTS

This entire series is dedicated to my devoted readers.

Thank you so much for investing your time and money on my stories.

If you have a spare minute, please leave a review online for any of the novellas you have read. It would mean a lot.

A big thank you goes to Nastasia and the team at Stardust Books for the wonderful artwork they produce for the covers of these novellas. As well as to my editorial team of Maureen Vincent- Northam, Brigit Taylor, and Deborah Longman.

Made in the USA
Middletown, DE
02 June 2024

55186336R00071